THE VALUE OF THE EMPIRE

THE VALUE OF THE EMPIRE
A King Montezuma Story

Book 3

Keith H. Adkins

ISBN 979-8-9895776-6-8
Printed in the United States of America
ChrisJen Publications
www.keithhadkins.com
Cover design by: ebooklaunch.com

Contents

PREFACE: An Aztec Synagogue 1

ACT I
Poetry in Tucson

SCENE ONE: Psalms 1-72 10
SCENE TWO: Psalms 73-150 34

ACT II
Wisdom in Tubac

SCENE ONE: Proverbs 57
SCENE TWO: Job 68

ACT III
Stories in Phoenix

SCENE ONE: Ezra & Nehemiah, Chronicles 81
SCENE TWO: Daniel... 102

ACT IV
Liturgies in Flagstaff

SCENE ONE: Lamentations, Ecclesiastes...................... 125
SCENE TWO: Solomon, Esther, Ruth............................ 146

ACKNOWLEDGMENTS.. 171
BOOKS BY THIS AUTHOR 172

PREFACE
An Aztec Synagogue

A phone call last week to the docent at the local Aztec synagogue went better than I could have hoped. Her name is Maria, and she told me that she is a Mexican of the Aztec faith, while most of her family became Catholic, so I immediately made an appointment to visit her on Saturday. I told her that I had been to Guatemala and Mexico to hear stories in context about the Law portion of the Aztec Scriptures. I somewhat did the same the next summer for the Prophets, but only experienced them from Monterrey, Mexico. I then explained that I was low on money, so now I needed to get creative with ways to experience the Writings section of the Aztec Scriptures. She was delighted with the request, because she said she loves to share about her faith and her synagogue. "I will look forward to meeting you," said Maria, "and will get started right away gathering ideas that might help you."

The week passed quickly because I was very busy with my job as a High School history teacher. On the day of the trip, Phoenix hit a balmy 100 degrees Fahrenheit for the first time this year. Hard to believe it's only April 21, but the record earliest 100-degree day was March 26, 1988. I haven't even opened my pool yet, because it's not about how hot it gets during the day, it's about how cool it gets overnight. Once the temperature stops dropping below 70, the pool becomes tolerable. Most people think I'm crazy for living here, but the pool makes a huge difference, and finding shade and a breeze are the other keys to a successful life in the desert. Sipping a coconut-lime drink doesn't hurt either.

The Value of the Empire

As I got ready for the short excursion downtown, I realized how fortunate I was to have a job that gave me the summer off. Sometimes I get so caught up in work that I don't notice the wonderful things around me. This morning I was noticing. The saguaros were beginning to bloom, but they were all over the main body rather than confined to the crown. I heard this unique phenomenon was due to the stress of drought and heat, but had never seen it. The West Indian Lantana was blossoming, an emerald green and scarlet red Elegant Trogon was sharing its song, and a coyote walked across my front yard. All in all, I thought it was a pretty hard day to beat.

The appointment with Maria was for 10 a.m. The traffic on the 101 was surprisingly heavy, and got worse on I-17 as I headed downtown. To be honest, I had never been in an Aztec synagogue, so I was mildly uncomfortable. After parking, I went in and was cheerily greeted at the front desk, then mentioned my appointment with Maria. The woman picked up a telephone and let Maria know I was there, so I took a seat, feeling much more relaxed.

A few minutes later a bubbly woman in her fifties, although I'm a terrible judge of age, came out and greeted me. "I was delighted with your call last week, and have some thoughts about how I can help." She then invited me to her office, and I followed her down a short hallway to a small room with a desk, two chairs, and lots of bookshelves. She sat at her desk and asked me to be seated. "So, first of all," she began, as she looked at her notes, "was your first trip to Mexico an attempt to hear all of the stories from the Law part of our Bible, while in their proper setting?"

"No, no," I said with a smile. "We just focused on some of the stories from Genesis 12 through 2 Kings."

The Value of the Empire

"So, who is 'we'?"

"Wow! Sorry. Guess I'm getting ahead of myself. Two years ago was the first trip. It was actually my son Jameson's 18th birthday gift, but I accompanied him. He is thinking about going into ministry, and my wife and I wanted him to see the origins of our Caldwellian faith. I hired Geraldo, a Mexican guide, who met us in Guatemala, and told us the stories where they took place, as we traveled to Mexico City.

"Thanks," she said. "That makes sense. I love it that you focused on the Law and the Former Prophets, because they tell a complete story from the forming of the empire to the exile."

"I'll have to give credit to our guide Geraldo. I just asked for the stories from the first five books, but he insisted that we cover the first nine books. I thought his plan would cover eleven books, but Geraldo explained that Samuel and Kings were originally two books, not four. The next summer, my wife joined the two of us for a trip to Monterrey, Mexico, where I shared the stories from the Prophets. Since Jameson and I already knew the sites of the former Southern Empire, we just needed to experience the former Northern Empire."

"Those remaining prophets," she explained, "are called the Latter Prophets. Isaiah, Jeremiah, and Ezekiel are further designated as the Major Prophets and the remainder are the Minor Prophets, also known as the Book of the Twelve." A smile grew across my face as I realized that Maria was just the person I needed to help plan the final experience.

"That's what brings me here. I'm looking for ideas about how to present the Writings section of the Aztec Scriptures to my son."

"Okay. Well, I think you'll be happy with my ideas. There are twelve books that are officially listed as Writings, and I've

The Value of the Empire

broken them into four categories: poetry, wisdom, stories, and liturgies. Among the most famous poems in the world are those by King Montezuma. They have all kinds of classifications, but they are all called Psalms. To enrich your appreciation of poetry, I would recommend traveling to the Universtiy of Arizona in Tucson. Call Paola Valenzuela, she's the Event Coordinator for their Poetry Center, and see if you can lead a one day workshop on the Psalms."

"Oh, my heavens! Not sure I'd feel comfortable doing that."

"When you called me last week, didn't you mention you're a high school teacher?"

"And?" I asked, while feeling a bit caught.

"If you love the Aztec Scriptures and you love teaching, you'll get over yourself."

After I laughed uncomfortably, she continued. "It really is a great place. Over a thousand poets have been invited to read their work at the center since opening in 1960, and the Dedication Ceremony featured a reading by Robert Frost."

"Okay, now you're just trying to scare me!"

"Not at all. I'm trying to motivate you. Besides, you wouldn't be teaching your poems, because they are Montezuma's." Then, looking mildly perturbed, she said, "Next I would recommend going to the small, historical town of Tubac. Have lunch at Wisdom's Café and soak up the conversations of the eclectic group that eats there. Try to engage some of them in conversation, because that's where I think you could discuss the books of Proverbs and Job."

"Love that idea. It seems much more natural."

"Good. Then I would visit the Nature Conservancy right here in Phoenix. They started in 1966 and have protected more than 1.5 million acres of Arizona land. They thrive on the power of story to get their message out, so that's where you could find a kindred spirit. There I would share four stories: Ezra, Nehemiah, Chronicles, and Daniel."

"How would I go about it?"

"That, my friend, is on you. Finally, I would go to Flagstaff and visit their Aztec Synagogue."

"Why not here?"

"This last part of the Writings have become liturgy for worship, and the Flagstaff synagogue has some wonderful copies of the original five: Lamentations, Ecclesiastes, Solomon, Esther, and Ruth."

"Wow. I can't thank you enough."

"Hold on. I'm not done." She then handed me a copy of *Don Miguel Ruiz'* book *The Four Agreements: A Toltec Wisdom Book: A Practical Guide to Personal Freedom.*"

"I like that book."

"I don't want you to like it, I want you to live it. It will help you on this final leg of your journey."

As I graciously took this gift, I shook her hand warmly and thanked her profusely. Walking back to the car I hoped to focus on driving, because so many things were going through my head. It will be exciting when Jameson returns home after his second year of college, and by that time I hope to have everything lined up for this summer's experience.

When I got home, I handed my wife the book. She smiled and said, "He's a favorite of my people. He's a *nagual*, who shared in this book the teachings of the Toltecs. It's a way of life that shows how to find happiness and love."

I sat down and started reading the book in earnest. It wasn't long until I realized why Maria gave me the book. The four agreements amount to a code of conduct that frees one up from wasting time on unnecessary things. They are:

> 1. Be impeccable with your word.
> 2. Don't take anything personally.
> 3. Don't make assumptions.
> 4. Always do your best.

As I contemplated the meaning of these words, and their application to the Writings section of the Aztec Scriptures, something important dawned on me. I realized that the book was about me, so that's how I could attempt to live the book, as Maria suggested. If I was going to lead Jameson through this final part of the Old Testament, I needed the rules to apply to myself. To be honest, it's much easier to impose the agreements on an inanimate object like the Bible, but Maria wanted me to live what it said. As a Caldwellian, I have always been focused on the teachings of Jim Caldwell, so my appreciation for the roots of his faith needed to be owned. This turned me to a study of the Toltec wisdom. If I could manage to understand how its wisdom guided the Writings, perhaps I could let the Aztec Scriptures speak fresh and new to both Jameson and myself.

Toltec wisdom is about knowledge. Those who practiced it came together as masters and students at Teotihuacan. Jameson and I visited those pyramids on our first journey to Mexico, to experience the sights and sounds of the stories from the Law and the Former Prophets. I also went online to www.am-innovations.com which says, "The Toltec System of Knowledge is a Practical Exploration of the Great Spiritual and Physical Universes, and as such is a Facet of the Diamond of the One Life." That thrilled me because Jim Caldwell is referred to as the Diamond. He rose from the dead from an old diamond mine, giving that dual message of love and eternal life. That said, Toltec knowledge didn't form a religion. Its practitioners appreciate all spiritual teachings which leads to happiness, and they practice it as a way of life.

Now I have one month to finish planning these outings. They will involve four, mid-week day trips to the locations Maria recommended. My first task was to call Paola at the Poetry Center and see if I could schedule a time to teach the Psalms. Even though their mission is to "advance a diverse and robust literary culture that serves a local-to-global spectrum of writers, readers, and new audiences for poetry and the literary arts," I didn't hold out much hope. To my surprise, and no little amount of fear and trepidation, she said "yes." June 18 was open, and before I knew it, Paola put my workshop on their calendar.

The trip to Tubac would be much more relaxed. I've been to the small, artsy town before, but Wisdom's Café is closed on Sundays and Mondays. They started in 1944 and are famous for their fried, fruit burrito and award-winning margaritas. It's a two-and-a-half hour drive to get there, so I'll plan to leave mid-morning and have lunch on the premises. Once the crowd thins out a bit, I'll see if I can engage some in a discussion of the wisdom of Job and the book of Proverbs. After looking over my calendar, I chose July 10.

The Nature Conservancy in Arizona began in 1966. Although they are undergirded by reports and data, they are driven by the power of story. They tackle climate change, protect land and water, and provide food and water. In Camp Verde, development and water scarcity were threatening a family farm, so the Conservancy upgraded their irrigation infrastructure. I thought it was a long shot to gain their interest in hearing four biblical stories, then I realized Ezra and Nehemiah were returning to Mexico after disaster. Chronicles was an intentional effort for denying problems, and Daniel was apocalyptic. Maybe this will work, I thought, so I called Daniel Stellar, the State Director, and he agreed to have a small group of his staff meet with me. He offered July 30 and I accepted.

The final trip would be strictly for learning. Jameson and I will go to the Aztec Synagogue of Flagstaff to hear about the last five books, commonly known as the Megillot. Maria told me that those books are used liturgically in worship for different holidays, and I found myself intrigued. Maria had already called the synagogue and got me lined up to spend the day with Atzi on August 13. Now all I have to do is study the other seven books, to do them justice when presenting, and most importantly wait for Jameson to get home for summer break.

ACT I
Poetry in Tucson

SCENE ONE
Psalms 1-72

"Let's get this show on the road!" exclaimed an enthusiastic Jameson, when we were finally ready to go.

His mother, Sol, gave him a kiss on the cheek, and my wife of twenty five years gave me a hug, as we headed to the car in our garage. Of course, we were only going to be gone for the day, but my class at the Poetry Center started at 9 am and the map showed we had a 2 hour and 18 minute trip ahead of us. We left before 6 to help avoid some rush hour traffic on interstate 17, and the trip south happily meant avoiding the bright, Phoenix sun in our eyes.

"Can't believe that cake mom made for me for graduating my sophomore year of college. She always goes above and beyond."

"Of course, but she would say it was from her Mexican culture of hospitality."

"How does that matter?"

"To your mother, she was doing the minimum, she was doing her best. You know, Ruiz's fourth agreement."

Jameson nodded and said, "That book was a fun read. Thanks for loaning it to me."

We cruised through the traffic with no delays, as the navigation system only showed normal slow downs. I just love science, but truth be known, I probably rely on it too much. As we drove past the airport, I noticed visibly fewer planes. Although 200 people are moving here every day, the busiest time is still the winter. That's when snowbirds arrive for a winter of golf, and masses arrive later on for the Cactus League spring

The Value of the Empire

training games. I must admit I was feeling a little anxious about this first opportunity, when Jameson broke the silence.

"That's a strange place," he said, as we passed the exceedingly strange sign that reads 'Rooster Cogburn Ostrich Ranch' in Picacho, Arizona.

"What's even stranger," I replied, "is that it is billed as 'The Darndest Place You'll Ever Visit.'" We agreed to never visit it.

Tucson was actually busier than Phoenix, but then again we were arriving at peak rush hour. The University of Arizona is in downtown Tucson, and the Poetry Center was easy to find. I was delighted to find a parking spot and before we knew it, Jameson and I were at the front desk. The facility didn't officially open until 9, but the kind woman there was expecting me. She escorted us to our room and said, "You have twelve people signed up for the one day seminar, and it's a great variety of individuals. Enjoy!"

We settled in to the fairly large room, put two 8' x 10' tables next to each other, and set up fourteen chairs around them. Feeling a little unworthy about teaching college students, I pulled the teacher's chair from the front desk and placed it at one end, as a sign of prominence. As the students arrived, and it was time to begin, I looked out and realized these kids were about the same age as my high school teenagers. Soon my anxiety abated and I began with, "Welcome to this seminar about the poetry of the book of Psalms. They were a collection of one hundred and fifty poems, composed from the time of King Montezuma to postexilic Mexico."

"Hey, prof," called out one of the students, "we're poetry students, not Bible scholars. What's postexilic?"

"Great question!" I said. "First of all, let me mention that I'm not a professor. I'm a High School history teacher who loves poetry and the Psalms. Also, this isn't a regular class, so feel free to be interactive. It's my hope that we can learn together. Any other questions?"

"Yes," said the same student. "What's postexilic?"

Several sarted laughing, and I felt a need to prove myself, so I said, "When Cortés and the Spanish conquistadors seized Tenochtitlan, which is now Mexico City, they deported the upper class Aztecs to Spain. That's known as the Exile. They were there for forty seven years, then Cyrus of Persia overthrew Spain and allowed the Aztecs to return home. Postexilic poems were those written when they were back in Mexico."

That seemed to help, then another student raised her hand and said, "I heard there were 151 Psalms."

"Very good. The Greek translation of the Aztec Scriptures is called the Septuagint, and it indeed had a 151st Psalm, but it was excluded during the canonization process."

It was surprising that nobody had a question about that statement, then I realized these kids were pretty sharp. I suspected they were simply testing me, and, if so, I think I passed their vetting. "The Psalms were finally written down for use in Templo Mayor, once it was rebuilt, and these poems were of great importance for ritual and liturgy in Aztec worship. As they were sung, they were often accompanied with dancing and music."

"Sounds like a party," suggested another, as the class loosened up with several people laughing in a good way.

"Very much so. To the Aztecs, worship itself was considered a holy day, and experienced as a holiday. The sheer joy of having their Temple rebuilt made for a phenomenal celebration, and that's what worship is. Here's one more comment as a means of introduction. There's a wide variety of classifications of the poetic psalms, and they were divided into five books to imitate the Law section of the Aztec Scriptures."

"That sounds like two comments."

There was a brief moment of silence, then we all laughed. It felt like we were off to a great start and I couldn't have been happier. Jameson looked comfortable sitting among students from the 'other' university, but I was glad he wasn't wearing his Arizona State University shirt. No need for in-state rivalry while I'm trying to teach. I then handed out a syllabus for the day so they could know that we wouldn't dwell endlessly on just a few psalms.

"The next chance you get, open a Bible to the first Psalm. In most versions it will start with the title, 'BOOK I: Psalms 1-41,' and the first two psalms introduce the entire book. Psalm 1 distinguishes between righteous and wicked people, while Psalm 2 differentiates between Mexico's king and other rulers. The first psalm is a didactic wisdom poem..."

A student immediately interrupted with, "Now that sounds like something that could be useful in the Poetry Center. What is it?"

"Didactic just means teaching, but the ulterior motive is usually moral instruction."

"Nope," said another. "Probably no value here."

After some mirth, I continued. "Wisdom isn't so much about knowledge, as it is about using experience to make good decisions." A female student suggested that she just might try to write a didactic wisdom poem about avoiding situations that could turn bad. "Wonderful," I said with an approving smile. "Just one other thing about the first two psalms."

"Yeah, right," the class said almost simultaneously.

I flashed a quick smile, then said, "Psalm 1 begins with a

beatitude, 'Happy are those...' and Psalm 2 ends with a beatitude, 'Happy are all....' These happiness sayings bracket the introduction to the Psalms, and no matter what the political climate might be at any given time, following the LORD is the right thing to do."

A young man raised his hand and said, "I sure wish I had a Bible to follow along as you go."

Embarrassed that it hadn't crossed my mind, I quickly called Jameson over and gave him my credit card. "Please find ten copies as fast as you can." Two of the twelve who signed up for the seminar never came, then the most surprising thing happened. Three of the students pulled out their Bible. "Well, some of you are more prepared than me." As Jameson was going through the door I called to him and said, "Make that seven." I then turned to the class and said, "Let's go ahead with the third Psalm while we wait."

A student asked, "What about the guy who just left?"

"Oh, I'm sorry. That's my son. If you're interested, we'll tell you why he's here during lunch break. Meanwhile, Psalm 3 is a lament. Do you know any lament poems?"

After a short silence, one student said, "*Lament for the Makers* by W. S. Merwin."

"*A Lament* by Percy Bysshe Shelley," said another.

"*A Writer's Lament* by Bill Munn," said yet another.

"Wow! I'm impressed. I actually found that last one when preparing for the class. It ends with, 'who can write again, the Iliad, or Macbeth, or maybe even the Bible.' I love that. Great poetry calls us to emote, and Psalm 3 is about placing one's trust in God in difficult situations."

"What do you call this coincidence?" a female asked as Jameson returned right then with seven Bibles.

The Value of the Empire

Jameson smiled and said "This Poetry Center is great! The woman at the front desk quickly rounded up all seven."

Responding to the young woman, I said, "I would call it good luck, but you call it whatever you want." Jameson then handed out the Bibles and I had everyone turn to the poem. "There's just one more thing I want to say about Psalm 3. Notice the word *Selah* at the end of each stanza? They all said, "Yes," so I said, "Any idea what it means?"

A young man said, "I heard it means *amen*."

"Yes. That's a very common understanding, but the fact is, it is such a rare word that nobody knows for sure what it means. Any questions before we move on?"

Another young man said, "Not a question, but I'd like to say that I'm inspired to write a poem of grief, because I've never thought of the Bible for source material."

That really did my heart good, so I said, "Thanks, so much! Broadening our horizons is what I think education is all about. Maybe this collaborative effort to teach the Psalms at the Poetry Center will pay off far more than I could have ever expected. Okay, let's turn to Psalm 8 and read it through before we begin discussing it." All but one opened their copy and quickly read the nine short verses. I asked the other young man if there was a problem, and he said he didn't know where to find it. I was delighted that nobody laughed, and simply said, "If you open it in the middle, you'll find it." He looked shocked when that worked, then I continued. "See the tag line 'according to the Gittith'?"

"What's that?" asked a young woman.

"Yeah, I don't git-tith it," said Jameson to a round of groans. Another suggested, "Maybe it's the King James Version." Some laughed, and I realized there was a pretty wide spectrum of biblical knowledge among this small group. "A gittith is probably a musical instrument," I said, "but scholars have found its identification to be elusive. The reason the psalm needed accompaniment was because it was written as a song. Can songs be poems?"

"Sure!" said another. "Chrissie Hynde wrote 'I'll Stand by You' for The Pretenders, and that song is definitely a poem."

All of a sudden I realized I didn't have names and faces put together, so I asked Jameson to go to the front desk again and see if we could get name tags. He quickly returned, and everyone wrote down their name and put the tag on their shirt. I immediately said, "Thanks Olivia," I know names are important, and since I'm a perfectionist at heart, I'm glad to get that little problem corrected. "Please look at verse 6 and tell me what you think about the word 'dominion.'"

Henry spoke up and said, "Sounds like a trick question."

"Unintentional, but you're probably right, so let me just talk about it for a moment. Many people of my age think it means that humans are to dominate, and have used that as an excuse to plunder the earth through mining. That is not at all what it means. It means that God set humans on the earth to be caretakers, and certainly not to dominate one another."

Emma quickly scribbled a note and said, "That's going to become a poem for me to write, and I hope I can do a reading of it some time here at the Center."

"Great! Here's another poetic song: Psalm 19. Take a few minutes to read through it, then we'll discuss it."

"So that's where that comes from," blurted out Sophia. "My pastor often says 'Let the words of my mouth and the meditation of my heart be acceptable to you, O LORD, my rock and my redeemer,' and now I know its Psalm 19:14."

The Value of the Empire

I said, "The Bible is probably referenced in every day life far more than most people realize. Now, if you like natural theology, that's what the first six verses are about. 'The heavens are telling the glory of God; and the firmament proclaims his handiwork.' For me, when I look up at the night sky, my mind drifts to thoughts of infinity and eternity. Likewise, this part of the poem celebrates God's glory in creation, but I want to draw your attention to the word 'God.'

Oliver spoke up and said, "If this seminar becomes religious, I'm outa here."

"Fair enough. What I want to point out is that the first six verses use the Aztec word *El* for God, and the next four verses use the Aztec word *YHWH* for God."

"Then who," asked Emma, "is the LORD?"

"When it shows up in capitals, it is giving you the clue that the word behind the translation is *YHWH*."

"I'm lost," complained Oliver.

"When the Aztecs experienced God as transcendent and far away, they used the term *El* for God. When they experienced God as close and personal, they used the term *YHWH* for God, because it was God's own name."

Evelyn said, "Please say more."

"Yahweh comes from Exodus 3:14, when God first reveals the divine name. The Bible is full of examples of God being both transcendent and personal and I think that's the point. God is whatever you need. Whether you need an overseeing protector or a relational God, the Bible has stories to support that."

"Now that sounds more like poetry. Thanks," said Sophia.

I said, "Let's try the 23rd Psalm," and that turned out to be familiar to most of them. After they quickly read it, I said, "It's obviously a very personal poem because it is bracketed with

LORD at the beginning and the end, and at the very center of the poem are the words, "you are with me" (vs. 4). God's overseeing protection and intimacy combine wonderfully in this poem of trust."

"I've had too many experiences of broken trust to be much of anything but a skeptic," said Mia with a frown.

"Thanks for sharing, Mia. That sounds very painful, so I hope Psalm 23 can inspire a useful poem for you. It involves a beautiful sheep/shepherd metaphor."

Sophia spoke up and said, "It kinda gives me the creeps, because I only hear this psalm read at funerals."

"Good observation. To help us all settle in for an enjoyment of the 23rd Psalm, I see this poem as a way of life more than a solemn song about death." Everyone smiled and nodded in appreciation. "Another great thing is that it's about God and a single sheep, not an entire flock. That's what makes it so personal."

"I don't believe in God," complained a distressed-looking Oliver. "When my parents died in a car crash, there was no magical deity to make a difference." The class sat in stunned silenced. It seemed like forever before Sophia finally got up to go over and give him a hug, but Oliver crossed his arms and would have nothing to do with it.

"I'm sorry," offered a choked up Emma, as Sophia returned to her seat.

"Not your fault that my parents died," responded Oliver in a cold-hearted manner.

After another moment of silence, Henry said, "I don't believe in a magical deity either, but I've got to admit that history has shown a preference for believing in something greater than ourselves."

The Value of the Empire

Oliver responded, "I only trust myself." The class was quiet yet again, so I finally asked if he had anything more he wanted to share. "Just stay with the poetry. That's why I signed up. I could care less where it comes from."

"Okay," I said, "let's bring the discussion back to poetry. Who is it that said, 'No man is an island?'"

Everyone pulled out their phones and googled it. "John Donne!" called out Noah. "An English poet who wrote it in his devotional book in 1624."

"It's another great metaphor," I said. "It shows what its like to be a human, by comparing a person to an island that's disconnected from other land." Oliver continued to sit with arms rather defiantly folded.

"Yah," said Sophia. "Don't be an island, be a sheep."

All of a sudden, Oliver sat up and said, "Wait a minute. Didn't you say the Aztecs used the term *El* for God, when that thing you call God is experienced as transcendent and far away?" I nodded a yes, and he said, "That's how I experience God. So far away I'm disconnected, or God is disconnected from me. Either way, leave me and my island alone."

"Okay, try this. Psalm 23 is a prayer," I responded.

"How does that make a difference?" Oliver asked.

"When we are in prayer, it's like being alone on an island in a conversation with God." Oliver returned to folded arms, and I went on.

"Now let's take a look at the rest of it. The poem starts with 'The LORD is my shepherd,' and that tells us a lot. Using LORD with all capital letters means Yahweh, which is God's name, and it indicates intimacy."

"Sorry, Dad, but that just seems a little weird," said Jameson, as others squirmed a bit in their seats.

The Value of the Empire

"I suppose folk of your age think of intimacy in terms of sexuality, but it's simply a feeling of connectedness. It can mean sexual, but here it obviously implies emotional closeness. The emotional closeness comes from the comfort that a personal God cares for an individual. Remember, this is a prayer by King Montezuma, as he celebrates experiencing God looking over him like a shepherd. The first verse ends with 'I shall not want,' which means that the king is content. Somebody want to read verse 2?"

Amelia offered, "'He makes me lie down in green pastures.' Now wait a minute. That sounds like a dominant male trying to force himself on me.'"

"Whoa, I never read it that way before, but thanks, Amelia. It's good to hear how different generations experience the Bible. Actually, the original Aztec word here is about helping animals lie down, which furthers the sheep-shepherd metaphor."

"Okay, then let me continue", said Amelia. "'He leads me beside still waters.' Even I get that. Some of my favorite memories are sitting by a lake on a calm day with my best friend. I guess it's an image of trust and rest."

Sophia then started to read the next verse. "'He restores my soul. He leads me in right paths for his name's sake.' Yes. I can testify that God has restored my soul, because he led me on the right path to Jim Caldwell."

"You all are about to lose me," said Oliver, in a threatening way, as he sank deeper in his chair..

"Interestingly, the Aztec word here isn't so much religious as it is about life. Oliver, have you ever felt refreshed?" That seemed to settle him down, but he didn't answer. "Now for the all important fourth verse. Let me read it and then we'll talk about it. 'Even though I walk through the darkest valley, I fear no evil; for you are with me; your rod and your staff—they comfort me.'"

"Doesn't happen," said Oliver emphatically.

"Isn't Hell 'the darkest valley'?" asked Sophia.

"Nope," suggested Mia. "I've been to hell, and it was called depression."

Several students agreed with her, then I said, 'It's about death, whether you're talking physical, emotional, or spiritual." I then turned in my Bible and said, "Here's how Job described the darkest valley: 'before I go, never to return, to the land of gloom and deep darkness, the land of gloom and chaos, where light is like darkness' (10:21-22)."

"Yep," said Sophia, "that's Hell."

"Nope," said Mia, "that's depression."

Oliver surprised everyone by saying, "It reminds me of a cave."

"What?" questioned Noah, with a bit of intrigue.

"Never mind him," suggested James. "He's into Plato."

Not being very well grounded in philosophy, I turned the discussion back to the Bible. "Truer to the text would be Isaiah 9:2: 'The people who walked in darkness have seen a great light; those who lived in a land of deep darkness—on them light has shined.'"

"Yep," said Sophia, "the light is Jim Caldwell!"

Jameson and I looked at each other for a moment, as if Sol was in our midst. "Let's move on to the 'fear no evil' part. Anyone able to do that?" Nobody spoke up, so I asked what the poem says about keeping fear at bay.

Evelyn, who talked for the first time, said, "'for you are with me.' I believe in God, but fear seems greater than God."

"Nothing is greater than God!" proclaimed Sophia.

The Value of the Empire

"I'm greater than God," announced Noah.

After a moment of silence, Amelia asked, "What do you mean?"

Noah smiled and said, "Because I'm nothing."

After some confused laughter I said, "Sounds like a Sufi or Rumi poem. Are you of Eastern religion persuasion?"

"Not particularly," said Noah. "I just like to learn from all religions. I believe sacred writings are worthy of study, consideration, and reflection."

"Great! Learning should never be restricted. The rest of verse 4 offers comfort through the sheep-shepherd image. So what do you think about verse 5?"

Mia offered to read: "'You prepare a table before me in the presence of my enemies; you anoint my head with oil; my cup overflows.' Who in their right mind would fix dinner for a bunch of enemies?

"We do that," said Sophia, "at my church. During communion and at pitch-in suppers."

Oliver asked, "So you willingly have enemies at your church?"

"We willingly have room for everyone," she responded.

"So," continued Oliver, "what's that overflowing cup all about?"

"I think it's poetry," said Mia. "It's seems like a metaphor for reconciliation and peace. What do you think, prof?"

I said, "If we let it be poetry, perhaps what it means to you is more important than what it means." After a thoughtful pause, I asked, "Someone want to read the 6th verse?"

Noah surprised everyone by standing up to read. "Surely goodness and mercy shall follow me all the days of my life, and I shall dwell in the house of the LORD my whole life long."

The Value of the Empire

After he sat back down, Sophia complained. "I though it ended with 'forever,' not 'my whole life long.'"

"That's another one of those pretty famous interpretations, but it certainly does not mean 'forever.' The poem is all about the here and now. That's why he hopes goodness and mercy will pursue him throughout his life, and he especially looks forward to finding security when he's in Templo Mayor in Tenochtitlan. Anything else?"

"No thanks, you pretty much ruined the 23rd Psalm for me," said Sophia, as she sank into her chair and folded her arms. Everyone started to laugh, but I noticed that Sophia was serious. I stole a quick glance toward Jameson, and he saw it, too, so I decided to give her time to recuperate by focusing on the next item.

"Okay," I said, "let's move on to Book II, keeping our back-and-forth discussions lively. That should take us close to the noon hour and then we'll break for lunch. This afternoon we'll wade through the poems of Books III, IV, and V. Book II goes from Psalm 42-72. Why don't you spend about five minutes looking them over and let me know the first one you'd like to discuss?"

After just a few minutes, Henry said, "How about that first one, Psalm 42?"

We all turned to it, and I said, "Interesting. This one was originally with Psalm 43, but they were separated in the canonization process."

"Sounds like my parents," groaned Mia. Shallow laughter disappeared into reality, and we once again moved on.

"This psalm is a lament about being so sick, the author wasn't able to make a pilgrimage to Templo Mayor."

"I thought all the Psalms were written by Montezuma," said

The Value of the Empire

a mildly annoyed Sophia.

"Some were, maybe even most, but this is a great example of how scholars realized they were not all by him."

"Why?" asked James.

"Oh," said a surprised Noah, "I bet it's because Montezuma wouldn't need a pilgrimage to get to Tenochtitlan. He lived there."

"And why do you think it used to be a part of Psalm 43?" asked Evelyn.

I got up, grabbed a piece of chalk at the blackboard, and drew a quick chart of how scholars think it used to be:

Stanza 1	42:1-4
Refrain	42:5
Stanza 2	42:6-10
Refrain	42:11
Stanza 3	43:1-4
Refrain	43:5

"I'm not sold," announced Mia, our resident skeptic.

"That's fine. I'm just saying what the scholars think, and that certainly doesn't mean it's correct. They further their thoughts with the fact that the two psalms have many linguistic links."

"I'm buying it!" announced Olivia.

"That's fine, too, so let's jump right in. Have any of you hiked Sabino Canyon in the summer?"

"Yah," said Noah, "but its nasty hot."

"Can you imagine being desperate for water, then finding a dry stream bed?

"That would be awful," said Emma.

"Verse 1 says, 'As a deer longs for flowing streams, so my

soul longs for you, O God.' As powerful as this kind of suffering is, it's not the point of the verse."

"Okay, I'll bite," said Evelyn.

"This prelude to the psalm represents the author's passionate longing for God."

"Getting too religious, again," complained Oliver, with his arms crossed in the usual manner.

Sophia quickly shot back, "Deal with it!"

Not wanting to lose focus, I said, "Then think of it as poetry. What does your soul long for?"

Noah said, "Learning."

"Yes, thanks. This class is about poetry. We simply use the Psalms as timeless examples of lyrical prose. Someone want to read verse 2?"

Amelia rose her hand and read, "'my soul thirsts for God, for the living God. When shall I come and behold the face of God?'" She then looked up and asked, "What does it mean to behold the face of God?"

"Scholars say it's a technical term for entering Templo Mayor," I said, "but frankly I don't get it."

"I love that," said Emma. "A man who doesn't have all the answers."

"James, would you please read verse 3?"

He quickly said, "My tears have been my food day and night, while people say to me continually, 'Where is your God?'"

"Ooh," said Oliver, "I like that. The people are taunting the author for failing to get help from God! More power to them."

"Please," said Olivia, "if you don't want religious connotations, why are you pushing them now?"

Amelia was getting a little frustrated, and said, "I agree, and because of that, I'm going to work on a poem about tears being my food."

"Good stuff," I said. "Verse 4 completes this first stanza with a memory of wonderful pilgrimages of the past. I'm sure you can relate to going home for the holidays." They all nodded, then I said, "Okay, now read the three refrains."

After a few moments, Noah said, "They're the same."

"That's another reason the two psalms are thought to go together. That just leaves us with stanza 2. Please read verses 6-10, then share with me their poetic power."

"Well," said Evelyn, "verse 6 is sad, but I know a lot of college students whose 'soul is cast down.' My roommate got a bad grade yesterday, and she was in a pretty bad funk."

Olivia said, "I just love verse 7, where 'deep calls to deep.' What do others think that's about?"

"Not sure," said Emma, "but I find it interesting that the poem begins with a parched soul, and now deals with thundering waterfalls and billowing waves. Maybe the deep troubles are calling for deep solutions. Just a second." Emma grabbed her pen and notebook and quickly wrote down a few thoughts. She then looked up and said, "I feel another poem coming on."

I then looked to Henry and asked if he had any thoughts. "You guys stop too quick," he said. "The next verse spells out the answer. 'By day the LORD commands his steadfast love, and at night his song is with me, a prayer to the God of my life.' I think religion is interesting, but I find it difficult to put into practice. For me, the psalmist is finding help in his distress. All of a sudden, 'deep calls to deep,' makes sense, because when the depths of my troubles cry out to the depths of the creator of the universe, inexplicably, God is there."

"What about when God isn't there?" asked Mia.

The Value of the Empire

"Oh, come on!" complained Sophia. "God is always there. Sometimes we just find it difficult to sense God's presence."

Wanting to get back to Henry, I asked, "Do you have any stories about God being there?"

"Really tired of this God talk," grumbled Oliver, but nobody paid attention to him.

"I've never told this story before," responded Henry, "but my first year here at school I thought about taking my life." He paused for a moment, and even Oliver turned to listen. "My parents live in New York, and I had no friends here. I'm an introvert, so it was difficult to get to know people. It was just a dark night, in my dimly lit room, and I was hollowed out with loneliness. School wasn't really working for me, so I started to think about ways I could go about ending it all. About that time there was a knock on my door and a group was going down the hallway inviting everyone to go out for dinner. That's when my 'deep' was unknowingly calling to the depths of God, and God answered. That group that night became the angels I needed." Henry stopped again and choked back some tears along with most everyone else, and then continued. "Verse 8 says, 'at night his song is with me, a prayer to the God of my life.' The song of that story stays with me in a comforting way, and now I'm trying to learn how to pray to the God of my life."

"I think you just did," said Noah, with several others nodding in agreement.

"And wow!" said Olivia, "That song, that prayer, that confession, whatever it was, will become a powerful poem. I can't wait to hear it at some future reading here in the Center."

Henry said, "I'll sure think about it. If it can help others, it would certainly be worthwhile."

"Thank you, Henry, for sharing that very personal story."

Henry appeared to be uncomfortable, so I decided to move on. I asked, "Any thoughts about verse 9?"

Emma said, "I'll write a poem about God being a rock. That somehow seems to be a nice, genderless way to talk about God."

Henry surprised me by saying, "'Why have you forgotten me?' might be a good way to start my poem. Then the bit about being mournful, 'because the enemy oppresses me,' is a great metaphor for loneliness." I wanted to encourage Henry in his lyrical interests, but Oliver interrupted.

"I can relate to verse 10. My anti-religious stance makes people think I have, 'a deadly wound in my body,' so maybe that's why, 'my adversaries taunt me.' Pathetic!" He then looked back down at the psalm and read the end of the verse, "'while they say to me continually, 'Where is your God?' Taunting people doesn't seem very religious to me."

"Then write a poem!" declared a frustrated Olivia.

"Okay, let's have a look at Psalm 66, then I'll take us all out to lunch." After a surprisingly spirited round of applause I explained, "This poem is about liberation." Emma was pleased to hear this, then I said, "And it was meant to be heard. Someone want to come to the front and read it?" Emma quickly volunteered, and while she came forward I said, "Start with verse 5."

"Come and see what God has done," read Emma. "Sorry, I don't see much liberation going on here."

"Read verse 6," I requested.

Emma looked back down at the page and read, "'He turned the sea into dry land; they passed through the river on foot.' Sorry, I'm not familiar with the Bible. I'm here for the poetry."

James said, "That is the moment in history that all of

modern day liberation is based on. It's after the Aztec people escaped from Guatemala, and dramatically found themselves caught between Lake Izabal and the approaching Guatemalan army wanting to take them back into captivity."

When James paused for effect, Amelia took the bait. "What happened?" He responded by telling her to reread verse 6. She said, "'He turned the sea into dry land; they passed through the river on foot.' They were set free from captivity, but what happened to the Guatemalans?"

Noah said, "They drowned. Maybe they'll have it better next time around."

Sophia frowned. "I don't believe in that reincarnation stuff."

Emma said, "Hey, I'm a feminist, but let's not deal with our differences. Now, tell me more about liberation."

I said, "Verses 10-12 moves the story from the remote past to the recent past. Would someone please read them?"

Amelia read, "'For you, O God, have tested us; you have tried us as silver is tried. You brought us into the net; you laid burdens on our backs; you let people rise over our heads; we went through fire and through water; yet you have brought us out to a spacious place.' I think I smell a poem coming on."

"In what way?" asked Emma.

"Being tested, going through trials, and getting caught up in a net. Feeling burdened, experiencing snobs who look down on me, getting judged through fire and water, then coming out of it in a spacious place. Yeh, I think I could find a poem in all of that."

"Thanks so much, Amelia. Verses 16-19 celebrate a personal story of liberation. Read it to yourselves, then we'll discuss it."

Very shortly, Oliver uttered a complaint. "'Come and hear,

The Value of the Empire

all you who fear God.' That's one of the reasons I'm against religion. Why would people want to fear the God they worship?"

"Well, Oliver, that translation has an unexpected twist. The Aztec word translated into English as 'fear,' is better translated as 'reverence' or 'honor,' as we are called to have toward our parents.'

"There you go," stated Oliver with increasing anger. "I don't know how to revere dead parents, and I definitely don't know who God is!"

"Couldn't that at least become a meaningful poem?" asked Henry. He quickly got his answer, as Oliver stood up, flipped his chair over, and shocked everyone by walking out. Sophia wanted to go after him, but several students said that he's angry like that all the time. She couldn't take it, so after a few moments she got up and went after Oliver.

When Sophia got back to the classroom, she told us about the conversation. "He said, 'Leave me alone,' and I responded, 'but I care about you.' He then said, with a surprisingly angry voice, 'No you don't. You don't even know who I am!' I started to reach out to touch him on the shoulder and said, 'But I would like to know who you are.' He brushed my hand away in an almost violent way, and then faced me with an angry look.'" At this point the class was listening intently. "He said, 'I'm warning you. Leave me alone!' He walked on ahead and I reluctantly returned."

"How do you feel about that?" asked Noah.

Sophia said, "Not so good, but at least I feel better about me. The only thing I could think of was Jim Caldwell, and his parable about the lost sheep."

Henry said, "Maybe this is like that moment when the Aztecs made it across the lake, but the Guatemalans drowned."

"And your point?" asked Emma.

"Some people move on, while others die because they can't escape their pain."

"Astute observation," I said, "but it bothers me that he left. Anyone else have anything to say?"

Sophia said, "I'll grieve our loss. I'm sure Oliver had more to offer us."

"I'm not so sure," suggested Henry. "He's a troubled person. I'm ready for the rest of the psalm."

"Okay," I said. "Well, the rest of the psalm is summed up with, 'and I will tell what he has done for me.' This is your invitation from the poetry of the Psalms to write about the things you have been liberated from. Any ideas what that might be for you?"

"I'm a creative soul," said Olivia, "and I learned as a child that it is okay to color outside the lines."

Henry said, "I'm a cautious type, so I just might pray for God to help me be more open."

"Men," announced Emma. Most people looked confused, so she offered an explanation. "I have been liberated from men telling me what to do."

James said that the experience with Oliver liberated him from needing to change people, while Sophia felt liberated to work harder at evangelism. Evelyn said, "I'm a seeker, and this whole seminar liberated me to work harder at understanding the Bible."

Noah said, "I really like Eastern religions, so I would say I feel liberated to delve deeper into the great unknown."

"I'm an agnostic," said Amelia, "and I feel liberated to question things even more."

After a bit of silence, Mia said, "I'm a skeptic, and Psalm

The Value of the Empire

66 taught me to look more for the good things in life."

"I'm humbled that the class has gone so well. Now, as I said, lunch is on me. What's your favorite haunt?"

After a little discussion, the class agreed on Graze. Sophia said, "It's really close. Just go west from here on East Speedway Boulevard. Pass North Campbell Avenue, then when you see Himmel Park on your right, make a left U-turn and it'll be on your right. Luckily we're getting there a little early, so the crowd shouldn't be too bad. The burger place is small, and so is the parking lot." Everyone quickly figured out how to carpool, then Sophia said, "See you there."

Jameson and I got in our car and hoped they weren't pulling our leg. After a surprisingly short distance, we found ourselves parked in the right place. It did seem like a hole-in-the-wall kind of dive, but the sign out front was inviting: Graze Premium Burgers & Fresh Cut fries. When we walked in, the class was already ordering their meal, and I was impressed that the staff would believe I was going to pick up the bill. We looked the menu over, and Jameson immediately went with the Graze Double with Cheese. He also ordered a regular size of Fresh Cut Fries and a Chocolate Shake. I've always loved food, but am finding that, as I get older, I can't consume as big of a meal. I ordered a Graze Single, and just as I was ready to order some fries, a gigantic basket of fries was being taken out to a nearby table. I figured I would be able to pilfer some of Jameson's fries, so I just ordered a fountain soda. The bill tallied higher than expected, but this teaching thing was as much for me as for the students who signed up.

Some of the staff had kindly pushed tables together for us, and we gathered for a great meal. The discussion was also enjoyable, and I was pleased how inclusive the class was,

The Value of the Empire

because Jameson and I really felt like we were a part of them. Sophia reminded that we offered to explain during lunch about Jameson's presence.

"I can handle that one, Dad. For my 18th birthday, my parents gave me a trip to Belize, Guatemala, and Mexico to enliven my understanding of the Aztec Scriptures."

"Wow! That's a great gift," said Sophia.

Jameson continued, "Dad joined me for the trip."

"So much for a great trip," declared Henry, and the class roared with laughter.

When things settled down, Jameson said, "and he hired a Mexican guide named Geraldo to tell the sacred stories at prominent pyramids along the way. We saw Tikal, Monte Alban, Chichen Itza, Tulum, Cholula, and the ruins of Tenochtitlan."

Amelia said, "I have no idea what you just said, but it sounds like fun."

"The best thing was swimming at Tulum."

"Okay," said Olivia, "I've heard of that."

"On that trip, we covered the Law and the Former Prophets, or Genesis to Second Kings. Last year Mom joined us for a trip to Monterrey. Dad told the stories of the Prophets section of the Old Testament, including Hernan Cortés' overthrow of Mexico. Today is the first stop for this third trip, as Dad is working to bring the Writings section of the Bible alive." They seemed impressed, and when we were finished with our meals, we returned to our cars, and looked forward to the afternoon session.

SCENE TWO
Psalms 73-150

Jameson and I were the first ones back, and I started to get nervous as we waited together in an empty room. I looked at the clock and could tell Jameson was feeling the same way. Finally they all came strolling in and apologized. Sophia said, "We decided to stop for some ice cream." I couldn't believe they were still hungry, but then they thanked me for lunch. This really was a great group of students, but my heart sank a bit realizing Oliver wouldn't be returning. I silently offered a quick prayer that he might find peace, and be liberated from his anger.

"Ready for Book III?" I asked, while strangely feeling like a carnival barker. They all nodded, so I said, "To get a sense of Psalms 73-89, I chose numbers 73 and 80. Let's turn to Psalm 73 to begin, and look at verses 1 and 28." Everyone dug right in and got started. "Notice that this psalm is framed by a confession of God's goodness. I think it's because the poem depends on faith as a means of dispelling envy of evildoers."

"Just a second," requested Noah. "At the beginning of the poem, it says 'A Psalm of Asaph.' What's an Asaph?"

"Not a what, but a who. Asaph is thought to be one of Montezuma's chief musicians," and Noah gave an approving nod. "The issue here is in verse 3, where the poet is envious of the happiness of the wicked."

"I can relate," said Amelia. "I don't know if I believe in God or not, but if there is no God, then why should I bother to be good?"

"The way I answer that question," said Noah, "is that I believe we are called to leave this world in better shape than we found it."

The Value of the Empire

"Good luck with that one," snarked Mia.

"Why so negative?" asked Sophia.

Mia almost barked back, "Because I'm envious of the happiness of the wicked!"

"Wow," I said. "Perhaps we can look at verses 4-12, and see if we can guide the discussion around the poem."

The class seemed okay with that, then Olivia said, "Looks pretty good to me: verse 4, 'no pain;' verse 5, 'not in trouble;' verse 6…wait a minute. It doesn't seem to fit: 'Pride is their necklace; violence covers them like a garment.'"

"Sure it does," said Sophia. "Just like verses 4 and 5, verse 6 also suggests impunity for their haughty ways."

"Noah smiled and said, "Sounds like inspiration for evil."

"Hey, Noah," called out James. "You fit in with verse 10. 'Therefore the people turn and praise them, and find no fault in them.'"

Reading ahead, Noah replied, "Still sounds good. Look at verse 12, 'Such are the wicked; always at ease, they increase in riches.'"

"So," asked Evelyn, "what's the point of all this?"

I explained that, "There's a famous Old Testament scholar named Walter Brueggemann, who suggests Psalm 73 is the theological center of the Psalms."

"Happy for Walter," said Mia, "but that's no help to me."

"Maybe it could be," I said, "if you let theology be poetic."

"Now we're talking," said Olivia. "That's what I'm here for."

I said, "When something is in the middle, it often has poetic meaning. In this Psalm, the first twelve verses identify the problem. The last twelve verses, 18-28, offer the solution, and the middle, verses 13-17 represent the turning point for the poet."

The Value of the Empire

"So, you're saying," questioned James, "that the turning point is more important than the solution?"

"Yes. One cannot practice a new way until they have turned from an old way. Just like there's no such thing as multitasking."

"Fake news," suggested Mia.

"Not according to science. Anyway, look at how the poet does it in verse 13, 'All in vain I have kept my heart clean and washed my hands in innocence.'"

"That's what happened at Jim Caldwell's trial," said Sophia. "Dmitri Ivanov washed his hands and claimed to be innocent of Jim's upcoming hanging." Her comment was met with silence, and it seemed everyone else was more interested in the poetics than the spirituality.

"At a deeply human level," I continued, "verse 16 suggests that reason is insufficient for theology."

"Now that has poetic significance," said Emma. "When I can't understand something, I seek something outside of my experience."

"Yes," said Evelyn. "That's when I turn to faith."

Noah said, "That's when I turn to Eastern religions."

I then mentioned, "In verse 17, the poet chose to turn to God, which, in turn helped him understand the problem of the evildoers."

"Which is what turned him around, right?" asked Emma.

"Yes. Then verses 18-20 reveal the divine undoing of the wicked, like verse 18's 'fall to ruin,' verse 19's 'swept away utterly by terrors,' and verse 20's 'on awaking you despise their phantoms.'"

"Thanks," said Emma. "Plenty of poetry there."

"Verses 21-28 show the mental, emotional, and spiritual well-being that has come to the poet through this journey. He sums it up for himself in verse 28 that happiness isn't about depending upon oneself, but upon God."

"I find wholeness," said Amelia, "by communing with nature."

Jameson then spoke up for the first time and said "College brings me wholeness."

Everyone seemed rather shocked to hear him talk. Olivia expressed appreciation for his thought, then asked, "In what way?"

"I find happiness in community, and my classes are doing that for me." Several smiled and nodded affirmatively.

"Let's move on to Psalm 88," I said, with the intention of keeping the focus on the text.

Noah said, "So, it's a 'Prayer for Help in Despondency.' That should be useful in today's world. Personally, I keep from becoming despondent by focusing on Buddhism. It centers me in peace."

"You don't use the Bible?" asked Sophia.

"Sure, but Buddhism isn't so much a religion as a philosophy. I like to learn from all wisdom, and yes, the Bible has some great teachings."

"I have a question, prof," said Mia. "The introduction to this Psalm also says, 'A Song. A Psalm of the Korahites. To the leader: according to the Mahalath Leannoth. A Maskil of Heman the Ezrahite.' What does that mean?" General laughter broke out in agreement.

"I don't know."

After some mildly stunned silence, Mia said, "That's quite refreshing."

"Coming from a place of more experience in life than this class has, I can say that life is better when you don't have all the answers."

After another bit of thoughtful silence, Jameson said, "I've never heard him say that in my whole life!" Lots of laughter settled us in, as we got ready to deal with the Psalm at hand.

"I love that it's called 'A Song,'" said Olivia. "Songs are certainly a part of poetry."

"Absolutely," I agreed, "and this is a pretty difficult poem to sing. The first two verses are a cry for help, and verses 3-7 describe how he feels. Verses 8-12 share a complaint, and verses 13-18 contain an urgent appeal for God's help. Let's try to personalize this poem by taking the next 20-30 minutes to write your own poem, as inspired by Psalm 88."

Everyone pulled out their laptops and began the task. I wanted to look outside, but this was an interior room, so I got up and went to God's great outdoors. It was a bit warm and humid for a summer day in Tucson, so I quickly found a bench in the shade. A gentle breeze blew across me, not unlike the way I feel when I'm being inspired by the Holy Spirit. That made me hope that the students would be inspired by this break from our day of learning. My mind quickly drifted off to memories of my last two trips to Mexico, so I pulled my phone out and set an alarm for fifteen minutes. A huge smile crossed my face as I recalled friendly exchanges between Jameson and our guide Geraldo. The traveling was a bit much, but the payoff was beyond anything I expected. Hearing Geraldo tell stories from the Aztec Scriptures while we stood at the very place they happened, was both enlightening and thrilling. Sadness slowly crossed my face as I thought about our second trip. My wife joined Jameson and myself on that journey, but she wasn't interested in this excursion. Sol said she would have been happy to go if we were returning to Mexico, but Tucson just didn't intrigue her. A terrible rattling sound pierced my peace enough to bring me back to the present. Reaching down to my phone, I turned the alarm off and headed back inside. About half the class chimed in with, "More time please." They didn't even look up, so I sat down and waited for the first person to finish. About five minutes later, Henry put his pen down.

"My poem is ready, and it's definitely a difficult song to sing. I wrote about that night when I thought about taking my life." His eyebrows furrowed as if to say he wasn't sure he was ready. Finally, he said, "If you want to hear it, I'm ready to read it." Everyone stopped writing, looked up, and listened intensely.

A Poem Inspired by Psalm 88

I cried for help,
    within the emptiness of my soul.
It reverberated like a tree falling in the forest,
    but no one was there to hear.
My soul was deeply troubled,
    because my loneliness had consumed me.
I felt forsaken by life,
    and thought there was nothing left for me.

Overwhelming feelings possessed me,
    like a rogue wave destined for my demise.
I felt shunned,
    but blame was of no use now.
My choice for seclusion was mine,
    and mine alone.

Sitting in darkness,
> my eyes ached with sorrow.
Then I saw myself sitting in the corner,
> like a scared little child.
Inaudibly I formed a question to God.
> "Aren't you also the creator of night?"
Deafening silence echoed back
> my final note of despair.

I wanted to say, "How will my life end?
> That's all I want to know,"
but the words just stuck in my throat.
> That's when unexplained noises
filtered to my ears.
> Thank you God for angels unawares.
They saved my life that night,
> and I am forever changed.

Henry's sharing was met with silence, and soon I noticed tears falling on several faces.

"So glad they came by," said Sophia. "Thank God."

Those sitting next to him patted him on the shoulder, and I asked if anyone else wanted to share. It became obvious that they were deeply touched by the poem, and just wanted to sit with the moment.

After a little while, Olivia said, "I look forward to sharing my poem sometime here at the Center. I'll need a lot more time to get it done."

"Okay, then maybe we're ready to move on. Book IV covers

The Value of the Empire

psalms 90-106, and I'd like us to take a look at 95 and 100." The class quickly turned their Bibles to Psalm 95 and read it through. "Let's try something different again. Spend about fifteen minutes preparing a report about the following verses: 1) Sophia, 2) James, 3) Emma, 4-5) Evelyn, 6) Noah, 7a) Amelia, 7b Mia, and 8-11) Henry and Olivia.

"What about me?" asked Jameson.

"Oh, for heaven's sake. How embarrassing. I'm sorry. Why don't you join Sophia for a report on the first verse?"

They all tore into the assignment with great excitement, and I could hardly wait to hear what they had to say. Fifteen minutes seemed like an eternity when just sitting and waiting, so I got up to take a walk around the Center. It really is an impressive building, designed as 'a progression toward solitude.' I moved through the building's meeting rooms, and experienced the intended gradual retreat to the peaceful library collection. There I found the 80,000 items housed in various galleries, and a bust of Robert Frost, who opened the Poetry Center with a reading. It also inaugurated a Reading and Lecture Series that has now heard over 1,000 writers. My head was filling with awe when I realized it was time to get back to my humble seminar.

Walking into the room I was pleased to find everyone still at work. When I asked how much more time they needed, we agreed on ten minutes. Feeling honored to have this unique experience, I walked around the circle and spent some time looking at what they were doing. Taking my seat, I said, "Okay, Sophia and Jameson, what do you have for us from the first verse?"

"Let me read it, because poetry is meant to be heard," said Jameson. I must admit I broke a little smile of pride as he began.

"'O come, let us sing to the LORD; let us make a joyful noise to the rock of our salvation!'"

Amelia asked, "How are you going to keep that from being religious?"

"You might be surprised," said Sophia. "It can be about liberation, like when the term was used during the Exodus wanderings."

"But that's still about religion," complained Amelia.

Sophia explained, "God says in Exodus 17:6, 'Strike the rock, and water will come out of it, so that the people may drink.'"

"So how is that not about religion?" asked Amelia, with deepening frustration.

She responded, "Think more about the rock."

"Okay, but how's that about liberation?" asked Henry.

Jameson said, "The world needs more drinkable water. The poetry becomes about ways we today can liberate the thirsty, by striking the rock of our hardened hearts."

"Ooh, he's good," said Olivia. "Hey, prof, your son just might be on his way to becoming an honorary U of A student!" Kind laughter broke out, then Sophia continued.

"Try this one from Job 24:8. 'They are wet with the rain of the mountains, and cling to the rock for want of shelter.' Here I find rock as a metaphor for people who want to fight homelessness."

"We sure have that problem in Tucson," said James.

"But the churches don't care," complained Amelia.

Sophia fired back, "Not all churches. Please don't lump people or churches together like that."

Being a good, agenda-oriented man like his father, Jameson charged ahead. "We just have one more example, and it's from Proverbs 30:18-19, which is itself a poem:

The Value of the Empire

> 'Three things are too wonderful for me;
>   four I do not understand:
>   the way of an eagle in the sky,
>   the way of a snake on a rock,
>   the way of a ship on the high seas,
>   and the way of a man with a girl.'"

Emma didn't like this one, so she said, "the way of a man with a girl is just like the way of a snake on a rock."

"Great," said Noah. "Sounds like you have a poem that needs written."

Oliva said, "As our favorite poet, Robert Frost, once said, 'Poetry is when an emotion has found its thought and the thought has found words.'"

The class seemed sufficiently satisfied, so I continued. "Thanks, Sophia and Jameson. Now let's hear about verse 2 from James."

Being pro-religion, he was excited to share his findings. "Let me read it first. 'Let us come into his presence with thanksgiving; let us make a joyful noise to him with songs of praise.' What I found was that 'presence' has to do with being face-to-face with someone. This Thanksgiving, I look forward to being face-to-face with my family."

"Sounds like a poem," said Evelyn, "for denigrating social media. There's nothing like being present with someone, and too many of my friends think sending an emoji from time to time is enough."

Henry spoke up and said, "Had I chosen to be present with people, I might not have gotten so depressed." That got a few appreciative nods, then Mia got up, took a piece of chalk, and made a happy face emoji on the blackboard.

The Value of the Empire

"What in the world do you mean by that?" asked a rather angry Henry.

She responded, "I'm defending emoji's. When I can't be there face-to-face, I find they're better than nothing."

Deciding that this wasn't the time to take on social media, I said, "Emma, what did you find out about verse 3?"

"I hated it, but here it is. 'For the LORD is a great God, and a great King above all gods.' One thing I liked about it was that it acknowledged other gods. What I didn't like was that it sounded like theology, and what I hated was its patriarchy. That said, I could easily write a poem about the evils of men holding power, versus the joy of matriarchy."

"That needs written, Emma," said Noah. "Plenty has been said, but plenty more needs done."

Sophia said, "In my church, we refer to the kin-dom of God, rather than the kingdom of God. Little ways to promote equality helps in this world of division."

"Thanks, Sophia," I said. "Okay, Evelyn, please share verses 4 and 5."

She immediately started reading, "'In his hand are the depths of the earth; the heights of the mountains are his also. The sea is his, for he made it, and the dry land, which his hands have formed.' To me, this is a confession of faith that God is the author of creation. The poetic element would be about protecting this glorious yet fragile environment. Personally, I most easily experience God in nature, so my poem would be a call to activism against the destruction of rain forests for the holy grail of profit."

Olivia said, "So your poem would be prophetic, spelled with a 'ph.'" Some laughed, but they all agreed.

"Looks like you're up, Noah, with verse 6."

The Value of the Empire

"'O come, let us worship and bow down, let us kneel before the LORD, our Maker!' I see this verse being about humility. While I prefer Eastern religions, I appreciate Jesus' call to deny ourselves. Bowing down before anyone or anything is to affirm something greater. This verse is a call to empty ourselves of self importance, and reach out for something beyond. I'll probably work on a poem about Vishnu, to help people understand a bit more about Hinduism, then Allah, from the Islamic tradition."

"Educational poetry, I like it," said Evelyn.

"Isn't that what Kaepernick was trying to do when he knelt during the national anthem?" asked Mia.

"Nah," said Noah. "He wasn't educating, he was protesting racial inequality."

"See where that got him?" asked James.

"Yes," said Jameson. "A visual poem that's still talked about today."

"Good one, grasshopper," said a smiling Noah.

"Okay," I said. "Amelia, what do you have to say about verse 7a?"

She read, "'For he is our God, and we are the people of his pasture, and the sheep of his hand.' Even though I'm an agnostic, I can appreciate the idea of being cared for. My poem is developing along the lines of our need for one another."

"Why do we need one another?" I asked.

"I'm working on it," she said with an impish grin, "but here at the very beginning, I'd say without friendship and/or fellowship, we can start to feel like Henry did." She then looked at Henry and said, "Hope no offense was taken."

Henry replied, "What I've found is that the lack of community becomes offensive to the soul."

The Value of the Empire

"Love it," said Sophia.

After a brief pause I said, "Mia, what did you find of interest about verse 7b?"

"O that today you would listen to his voice!" she read. "Sounds like a rather angry rebuke. Religion and politics have a tendency to get out of hand, so I'm working on a poem about listening to whatever voice you want. For me, the problem comes when we expect everyone to hear things the same. I'm thinking about titling it, 'They,' which is the nastiest and most divisive word in our language. We need to let people be, and maybe that could move us toward unity." After a thoughtful applause from the class, I asked Henry and Olivia to finish us up with verses 8-11.

Olivia started by saying, "Verses 8-10 are simply about the Exodus from Guatemala, as the Aztec people journeyed to the Promised Land of Mexico. My interests focused on verse 10 that says, 'They are a people whose hearts go astray.' I'll definitely write a poem about following unhealthy paths, and talk about the values of diet and exercise."

Henry seemed a bit subdued as he began to talk. "It was troubling to me that God would say to his people, who wandered in the wilderness for forty years, that he loathed them. My poem will be about my personal journey to the Promised Land, and my fear that I may not be able to enter when I get there."

Some liked what Henry had to say, and others didn't. I realized he was going in a religious direction, so I said, "We're ready to finish Book IV by first looking at Psalm 100. It's titled 'A Psalm of Thanksgiving,' but more importantly it's categorized as a hymn. We have a chance to let this poem become a song by singing it, so take a few minutes to find our best singer, and we can all sit back and experience it."

The Value of the Empire

They quickly tackled the assignment, and found two volunteers. Sophia sang in her church choir and had a nice soprano voice, but Noah was a great tenor. As the class tried to decide who should sing the poem for them, I suggested they try a duet. Noah said, "I love to harmonize, so if you," speaking to Sophia, "could make up a tune that goes with the lyrics, I'll follow." They asked to leave for a few minutes to practice, and excitedly walked out. A moment later Noah came back in to get his Bible, saying, "Tough to have a song without the lyrics."

We could hear them practicing down the hallway, and were quite eager to hear how the song would work out. They took much longer than I wanted, but when they walked back in, Noah started with a lot of enthusiasm. He said, "We have titled this song, 'Make a Joyful Noise,' but first we want to teach you the refrain, verse 4. Don't look it up in your Bibles, because we want you to learn it. I'll sing it first, then you try it." After a hit and miss effort, he proceeded a line at a time and the group echoed them back. "Enter his gates with thanksgiving." The class tried hesitantly, so Noah said, "Come on, its just five words." One more try and everyone was loosening up. "The second line is 'and his courts with praise.'" They got that so he shared the third line, "'Give thanks to him, bless his name.'"

Sophia took over and asked if anyone had rhythm. After a bit of laughter, Evelyn said that she would give it a try. "Okay, just drum on your desk as you feel the beat. Everybody else just clap your hands with a joyful noise." Sophia then sang the full refrain with Noah doing harmony, and Evelyn covering percussion. Then they tried it with the class clapping their hands, and a little applause broke out after they successfully completed the refrain.

Sophia continued with, "Noah, Evelyn, and I will do the first verse, then you come in with the refrain when I point to you. Actually, we will sing the first two verses, but that's beside the point." They managed it quite well, then Sophia said, "All right, we'll lead the first two verses, then you sing and clap the refrain. We'll sing verse 3, followed by the refrain, then verse 5 and the refrain. Ready?" The class nodded their heads yes and off they went. It really became quite a joyful noise, and the class gave a standing ovation when it ended. That's when I realized poetry was just like music. Notes and letters are little more than symbols on paper. They both needed to be heard to be fully appreciated.

When they were seated, I said, "Now that's what the psalms were written for! They were designed to be music to the ears, so that they might touch the soul." Jameson looked rather proud, as the class just had an unforgettable experience together. When our eyes caught one another, I just knew Jameson was saying, 'and that's community.' Amelia, our resident agnostic, even said that she just found a new appreciation for the Bible.

After relishing the moment, then looking at my watch, I said, "The afternoon is passing quickly, so let's get into Book V. I want to start with Psalm 118 because it's a victory song, and I hear your basketball team is pretty good."

"Woot, woot, woot!" called out several of them, as they churned their firsts in the air.

After smiling, I said, "Look at verses 2-4. Think of them as cheerleaders giving directions to different parts of the arena. Verses 5-9 are like expressing confidence in the coach. Consider verses 10-18 as describing a difficult game that ended in victory, 19 to 25 as a flashback to waiting to get inside the arena, and 26 to 27 as a celebration upon admission. Verse 28 serves as a closing act of thanksgiving."

Olivia, the creative one, offered to kick it off. "Give me a 'U,'" she said while facing the north, and that part of the class responded with "U." She then turn to the east and said, "Give me an 'of,' and that part of the class said, "of." Facing south she said, "Give me an 'A,' and they dutifully echoed it back. Then she said, "What have you got?"

Before she finished the word 'got,' Jameson called out, "No idea. I attend Arizona State," and the class roared with hilarious approval.

After that, Sohpia said, "I'll paraphrase verses 5-9:"

> Coach wasn't happy with his last job,
>   then he found U of A, or U of A found him.
> He said, to allay fear, 'What can they do to me?
>   I will make this a winning team,
> and the students will have confidence in me.'

Something felt wrong, so I cautiously said, "Please remember, this isn't a legitimate interpretation of scripture, but it works to inspire poetry."

They nodded, then Henry said, "I'll give verses 10-18 a try."

> The Wildcats were surrounded,
>   with time running out.
> Then a guard fell from a hard foul,
>   and the free throws fell through the net.
> Victory was assured and new hope was born.

"I'll never forget," said Mia, as she immediately jumped into verses 19-25, "waiting outside McKale Center. We chanted to gain entrance, then the doors finally opened. The crowd broke into, 'This is the day that the coach has made; let us rejoice and be glad in it.'"

"Wow!" I said. "That almost returns to interpretation."

The class laughed, then Noah said, "26-27 feels like a benediction, so try this. 'Blessed is the one who comes in the name of the coach. We bless you from McKale Center because Coach has given us hope, so let's party.'"

A round of cheers went up, and I got a little nervous that we might be asked to quiet down. After all, the Poetry Center has a library in it. However, I didn't say anything, because we were having too much fun. "Let's move on to our final psalm, number 133." There was a surprisingly audible sigh of disappointment, which made me feel good and bad at the same time. "It's just three verses long, so will someone please read it for us, to get it off the paper and into our imagination?" James began:

> How very good and pleasant it is
> > when kindred live together in unity!
> It is like the precious oil on the head,
> > running down upon the beard,
> on the beard of Aaron,
> > running down over the collar of his robes.
> It is like the dew of Hermon,
> > which falls on the mountains of Zion.
> For there the LORD ordained his blessing,
> > life evermore.

"I don't get it," complained Amelia, "and the other psalm was much more fun."

After acknowledging what Amelia said, I suggested that we

just might have to dig deeper to find the treasure in this psalm. Then I said, "The first verse isn't too difficult, because it is simply about community. "Verse 2 harkens back to Exodus 29:7—'You shall take the anointing oil, and pour it on his head and anoint him.' That's a description of the anointing of a new chief priest among the Aztecs, and the overflowing image comes from Psalm 23:5—'You prepare a table before me in the presence of my enemies; you anoint my head with oil; my cup overflows.' All of this is a simile for community."

"Then what's the 'dew' business from verse 3?" asked Noah.

"It," I said, "creates another simile for community, because dew covers everything, same as an anointing. The last part of verse 3 is a reminder of the covenant God made with his people, the Mexicans, for life evermore."

"So how do we use this psalm poetically?" asked Olivia.

"Thought you'd never ask," I said with a smile. "I've compared it to the stages of community-making, developed by M. Scott Peck in his book *A World Waiting to Be Born: Civility Rediscovered*."

"Who's that?" asked Amelia.

To be honest, I was so dumbfounded that it took me a moment to recuperate. "Maybe you know him better from his bestselling book, *The Road Less Traveled*."

"Nope," responded Mia.

Still reeling, I began to think that many in this age group probably had no idea who George Harrison was. "Okay, fair enough. The stages of community-making can be noticed by somewhat discernable movements. Those stages have been given many names, but I like the four-fold evolutionary names Peck prefers of pseudocommunity, chaos, emptiness, and community."

"What's that got to do with Psalm 133?" asked Sophia.

"I'm getting there." Something told me that it was probably a good idea to have this be the last psalm, not to mention that I was getting a bit tired. The class had done remarkably well so far, but I could sense we were all just about done for the day. Ignoring this realization, I pushed on with my agenda. "First of all, let me explain the stages:

> 1) pseudocommunity—this is when people tend to speak in generalities and ignore individuality. It is fine for the short term, but its main purpose is to follow manners. A group can move on to the next stage by personalizing their comments.
>
> 2) chaos—this is when people begin to take sides. Group members try to heal or fix each other, and it's a win/lose process that gets nowhere. The only good thing about this stage is that division is better than the pretense of harmony.
>
> 3) emptiness—this is when people try to build bridges instead of walls, by letting go of expectations, prejudices, and solutions. It is a stage of very hard work, where the group members empty themselves of everything that stands between them and community.
>
> 4) community—this is when people find mutual support for a shared vision. They choose to resolve conflicts rather than avoid them. The shift is momentary, and a sense of peace pervades the room.

"Now I'm going to show how the psalm itself reveals the stages of community-making, and I hope this is where you find inspiration for poetry. Verse 1 is pseudocommunity, because unity here is little more than a hope. Verse 2 represents chaos, because finding a new priest/pastor is a challenging process. Verse 3a reveals emptiness, because community can't genuinely form without personal sacrifices. Verse 3b is that elusive thing known as community, because conflict resolution is short-lived. Have any of you ever experienced the peace that comes from the time when genuine community happens?"

"I did," said Sophia, "toward the end of a week of church camp."

"Did it last?" I asked.

"No, and I always wondered why I couldn't keep that feeling."

James said, "I found it after a week of mission work in Mexico, helping to build a home, and no, it didn't last."

"The church tries to build community each year," I suggested, "through the experience of Holy Week."

"I'm intrigued," said Noah.

"Good, but understand that I'm not trying to push my Caldwellian faith on anyone." I looked around, and seeing no objections, I continued. "Pseudocommunity is kind of like Maundy Thursday."

"What's that?" asked Emma.

"It's the night when Jim Caldwell gave the commandment to love one another, and instituted what Caldwellians call The Last Supper."

"So how is that pseudocommunity?" asked James.

"Because the disciples of Jim were willing to be loving, but unbelievably challenging times were ahead. Chaos is represented by Good Friday. The world has rarely known a deeper sense of chaos than the killing of a beloved leader, in this instance it was Jim Caldwell."

"Why do Caldwellians call that good?" asked Mia.

"Because it sets up the next stage of community-making, which is emptiness."

"Not seeing the connection," complained Mia.

"Emptiness reveals what Holy Saturday is all about. It foreshadows an empty tomb."

"Ooh," said Olivia, "emptying myself out is how I always prepare myself to write poetry."

"Community is what is found in Easter Sunday. It's an elusive thing, so people gather and sing and experience the mysterious moment when Jim rose from the dead."

Emma then asked, "Can we try to make sense out of the community-making process from this class?"

"Definitely pseudocommunity when we started," said Noah, "because we didn't know one another."

Sophia said, "I felt the chaos stage when Oliver stormed out of the class. As a church-goer, it made my heart ache."

"Emptiness might have been experienced when we returned from lunch," said Henry.

"Say more," I requested.

"If that stage is about building bridges instead of walls, then I saw letting go of the Oliver concern as a way of letting go of solutions."

Evelyn said, "And community happened when we applauded after the basketball-oriented psalm. Which one was that?"

"It's Psalm 118," said Noah. "I'll never forget that one, and I'm guessing that's why sports is so popular. At least when you're winning, because it gives that momentary excitement that 'teach' calls community."

The Value of the Empire

"Here's another moment," I said. "Class is finished." All of a sudden I thought of Good Friday, but that's beside the point. The class applauded, and one by one they shook my hand and thanked me. I suppose it's because they knew I didn't get any money. When they were gone, Jameson and I picked up our few things and left. We talked a bit on the way home, but somehow the experience just needed to marinate.

The Value of the Empire

ACT II
Wisdom in Tubac

SCENE ONE
Proverbs

The time passed quickly, while I put together some thoughts for our next trip. Finally, we stepped outside into one of those famous 115 degree summer days in Phoenix. Jameson and I said our goodbyes to Sol and headed off. We didn't have any set time for an arrival, because the customers and staff had no idea we were coming. My plan was to enjoy lunch, then see if anyone wanted to discuss the wisdom of Proverbs and Job. Wisdom's Café seemed like the ideal place, and my mind was filled with hope.

Two hours later, we drove past Speedway Boulevard in Tucson. Jameson and I just smiled at each other from our shared memories of the wonderful time at the Poetry Center. Next, we curved away from I-10, to head south on I-19. It was only about 45 miles further, so we pulled into the little, artsy community by late morning. Jameson committed the cardinal sin when he called it 'Two-Bach,' so I quickly informed him that it was pronounced 'Two-Back,' as in one step forward and two back.

The town is full of history. Being Arizona's first European settlement, it was established in 1752 as a Spanish Presidio. In 1775, an expedition led by Lieutenant Colonel Juan Bautista de Anza, marched through Tubac on his way to settle Alta California, and founded San Francisco. The Tubac Presidio State Historic Park and Museum does a great job of maintaining the treasured history of this small, unincorporated community.

"So where's Wisdom's Café?" asked Jameson.

"A few more miles down the road in Tumacacori."

The Value of the Empire

"Tuma-what-ori? That's weirder than Tubac."

"It's named after the nearby Tumacacori mountain range, but you can't get there from here." Jameson just shook his head in silence. "Wisdom's Café is on the frontage road, so we have to go past it, get off the interstate, and come back north. The good thing is we'll go past the Tumacacori National Historical Park, which protects the ruins of three Spanish mission communities."

"Great, but I'm ready for some lunch and wisdom."

We pulled into the parking lot and found the place surprisingly busy for a weekday. It hadn't changed since my last visit, and I was looking forward to their always excellent food. Jameson wasn't impressed by the large chicken statue outside, but I calmed him with the thought that this place really was eclectic, and that was why I hoped to find some interesting wisdom. We were seated at a nice table and chairs, and enjoyed viewing the rifles, hats, and guns on the walls.

"This place sure keeps busy," commented Jameson as he looked over a menu. "They have live music every Friday and Saturday, two-for-one margaritas every Tuesday, and a fish and chips special every Friday. They must be doing something right, to keep the customers interested. I'm going to go wander around a bit." I watched him look at antiques, paintings, murals, photos, medals, pottery, and countless treasures. When he got back to the table he said, "Okay, dad. You win. If the customers are half as eclectic as this place, I'm guessing we'll hear some interesting wisdom."

A middle-aged woman, wielding a pen and order pad, arrived and spoke with a detectable Spanish accent. "Can I get you boys an appetizer or something to drink?" We both requested a soda, and I chose a Shrimp Ceviche appetizer to share. Jameson mentioned he was pretty hungry, so when she returned he ordered the Combo Plate, and I chose a bowl of Pozole with a side of Mexican Rice. I then asked if I could talk to the manager.

"Something wrong?" she asked, with a bit of a scowl.

"Oh, no. I just want to see about approval to talk to some of the crowd when they begin finishing their meals." She gladly took me back to the kitchen, where I met Herb Wisdom, a stocky guy with a receding hairline and full mustache.

"So that's how this place got its name!" I said with an embarrassingly large amount of shock. Herb smiled and gave me a quick rundown of the five generations of Wisdoms who have run the place since 1944. His short talk showed an equal amount of joy and pride.

"So what can I do for you?"

"I'd like to gather some wisdom from your diners. Is there any place I can engage some in a discussion of the wisdom of the books of Job and Proverbs?

Herb smiled and said, "Sounds just like the kind of thing my diners would like." Herb gave his approval, and said I could lead the discussion from the live music area, since it's only used on Fridays and Saturdays. Returning to my seat, I was beaming, and the food had just arrived.

Jameson said, "You sure seem happy to see the food."

"Well, yes, but even more so because the owner gave me the green light to talk." I then dove into my hominy soup, while Jameson scratched the surface of his gigantic, meaty, Combo Plate. We were eating right along when I noticed the cup of ceviche, and was delighted when I tried it, because it's difficult to get good seafood when you're this far from the coast. I started looking around and noticed a few people finishing their meal. It was probably too early, but I wanted people to have time to think about what I wanted them to do.

I stood up and clanged my glass of soda with a spoon. "Excuse me," I called out, with the experience of a high school teacher. When I finally got most of their attention, I said, "Herb Wisdom has given me permission to do something." I thought a pregnant pause here might generate some intrigue, but this eclectic crowd was beyond that. "So I wanted to let you know about it. In about ten minutes, I'll be on the music stage leading a discussion of wisdom, for any who want to participate. It'll take place in two parts, and you are welcome to stay as long as you like. The first part will be about wisdom from popular proverbs and the biblical book of Proverbs. The second part will be a discussion of wisdom that can be gleaned from the biblical book of Job. Thanks for your attention." I then dutifully returned to my seat and everyone went back to dining. Not feeling too sure of myself, I asked Jameson what he thought.

"It was fine, Dad, but do you think anyone will participate?"

"That's the $64,000 question."

"What?"

"Never mind. I think most places would have ignored me altogether, but I have hope for this environment." I started looking around and saw that many people were digging into their desert order of 'The World Famous Fruit Burro.' I was getting a bit anxious about timing, but decided to wait out the full ten minutes. It felt like an eternity, but I finally walked up to the stage. My heart sank as several got up and left, but then I saw a good crowd wiping their mouths and turning toward me.

"What a great place to talk about wisdom. Thanks for staying, and I hope we can all get something out of this." Something I wish I had was my soda. My throat was dry, but I decided to wait until break time.

"We need more wisdom these days," called out a short man in a cowboy hat. "But first, whatcha mean by wisdom?"

"Many people think it's about knowledge, so therefore, only well-educated people can be wise. Obviously, that's not true. Sometimes it just boils down to good sense. The wise person puts their experience into practice, from whatever knowledge they have attained."

"Some of the dumbest people I have ever known have doctoral degrees," proclaimed a well-dressed man in the back.

"If it's not too intrusive, may I ask what you do?"

"I'm a professor at the University of Arizona," and the crowd roared their approval.

"Okay, we're off to a great start. Now I'd like someone to call out a popular proverb."

"Many hands make light work," offered an older woman at a table that appeared to be her family.

"She always says that when chores are needed around the house," said a young boy next to her.

I asked, "And where is the wisdom in that proverb?" There was a surprisingly thoughtful silence before one of the servers spoke up.

"I love working here. Its family, and we care about one another. I used to work in Tucson, and somehow I was always the one needing to pick up the slack."

Another older woman said, "There's a four-letter word for that." The crowd showed concern about what she was going to say next, because there were plenty of younger ones in the Café. Then she said, "The word is," spelling slowly, "L- A- Z- Y!" The crowd actually clapped their support.

"Okay, now for a biblical parable. Here's one from

The Value of the Empire

Proverbs 10:11. 'The mouth of the righteous is a fountain of life, but the mouth of the wicked conceals violence.'"

A man close by said, "I have a problem with that, because I think wickedness is in all of us."

I asked, "And where is righteousness?"

"In all of us," called out the professor.

"So where's the wisdom in this proverb?"

After a useful period of quiet, a younger woman said, "Water is certainly an image of life, so why shouldn't we all choose to follow our righteous life-giving side, rather than our wicked violent side?"

"I'll drink to that!" said a rough looking older man, who then got up, swigged the rest of his beer, and walked out. The crowd seemed happy to see him go, so I went right ahead and asked for another popular parable.

"Don't judge a book by its cover," said a man who had been sitting with the man who left.

"Very good. I suspect you have a reason for saying that one."

The man was hesitant for a moment, then said, "You never know what's going on in a person's life, but I'll tell you that my friend, who walked out, recently lost his wife." This eclectic crowd was hushed from the power of a parable.

After a few moments, I said, "Thanks for sharing that. It's an important thought to remember. Now, here's another biblical parable: 'Where there is no guidance, a nation falls, but in an abundance of counselors there is safety.'"

"Where's that found?" called out a younger man.

"Oh, sorry. It's from Proverbs, chapter 11, verse 14."

"I disagree," said the same man who had a problem with the first biblical parable.

The Value of the Empire

"That's great!" I exclaimed. "Because I see the Bible as something to interact with, not to force compliance."

"I think I like that," said an older woman in hippie-type clothes.

Looking at the man who disagreed, I said, "Tell us about how the parable affected you."

"My problem is more with the second half. Just because a governing body has an abundance of counselors, doesn't mean everything will be alright. They might have bad advisers."

"I like the first part," said Jameson. I must admit I was a bit surprised to hear him speak up. "Guidance is kind of like a lighthouse. When a boat is near trouble, it has a tendency to sink if there is no help."

"Thanks. Somebody have another popular parable?"

"How about," said a junior high-aged girl sitting with her family, "Actions speak louder than words."

"And why is that important to you?"

"I like to talk, and everybody throws that stupid parable at me at school. It made me so mad that I actually talked to my parents about it." Some careful laughter broke out when the people saw her parents were smiling, then she said, "They cautioned me about talk being cheap. I said that didn't help, so they said something strange about character. That didn't help either, but then Dad said that things don't get done by words. Now that started to make some sense. Getting my bed made in the morning doesn't happen by just saying I will make my bed. Unfortunately, it takes action." The crowd gave a sympathetic 'aww.' She continued, "And then Mom and Dad said that backing your words with action is what develops character."

That was a pretty hard act to follow, but I pushed on with a biblical parable. I had memorized my first two scriptural texts,

The Value of the Empire

but went ahead and opened my Bible to the bookmark. "Let's try Proverbs 12:22—'Lying lips are an abomination to the LORD, but those who act faithfully are his delight.'"

"Lies are an abomination to me, too," said a man who explained that he was a business owner in Nogales. "I ordered from one particular company, I won't even waste my time mentioning its name, and they lied about the delivery date. I started checking back with them every week, and they kept saying it was delayed. After a couple of months, I asked for the manager, and he said it quit being made last year! To say the least, I was furious. I tried to get somebody, anybody, to be held accountable for the lie, and he just protected his employees."

"Faithfulness is what it's all about for me," said another. "I spent twenty years in the US Marines, and our motto is 'Semper Fi,' which means 'Always Faithful.'" He then looked over at the Nogales business man and said, "You had a tough one. The boss was trying to be faithful to his employees, but they weren't being faithful to the customers. I suppose it's easier in the armed forces, because the commitment to fidelity is based on the assumption that your commander is trustworthy. The idea of 'employees' being unfaithful to the American citizens is unthinkable. So, I kinda like the proverb that, 'those who act faithfully are his delight.'"

"You all are making the Bible shine today," I said with a huge grin. "How about another popular parable?"

"Beauty is in the eye of the beholder," came a voice from the back of the dining room.

A guy with one of Wisdom's award-winning margaritas stood up, lifted his drink high in the air and said, "I always thought that was, 'Beauty is in the eye of the beer holder!'"

Uproarious laughter broke out, interrupted by someone

yelling, "That's not even a beer!" I waited quite a while for things to settle down, then asked what the parable meant.

Another man stood and said, "I've been to Barcelona, Spain and saw Sagrada Familia. You know what I'm talking about right?" Most in the crowd said, "Sure," then he continued. "Well my wife thought it was the most beautiful thing she had ever seen, but I thought it was gaudy."

I said, "That's a great example of the parable. Now let's try this biblical proverb from chapter 13, verse 16: 'The clever do all things intelligently, but the fool displays folly.'"

"I never equate clever with intelligence," said a middle-aged man. "It was always the clever person at work who was very calculating in what he did, and it was rarely nice."

"That's why," I explained, "intelligence is an important part of the story, but where does wisdom fit in?"

"It fits in," said an older woman, "when you allow intelligence to be more important than cleverness." The crowd was quiet for a bit, then people slowly started standing and clapping. It was a memorable moment that told me we should wrap up our discussion of Proverbs fairly soon.

"Let's try one more proverb, take a quick break, then have a look at the wisdom from the book of Job. Who's got another popular proverb for us?"

An older woman said, "The grass is always greener on the other side of the fence."

"And what is the wisdom of that proverb?"

She said, "I heard a sermon one time that 'twenty percent' was the answer to the question of 'how much more money would you need to be happy?' The answer was the same up and down the economic spectrum. In other words, it didn't' matter how much money you made, it was never believed to be enough. I kind of think that's an example of the loss of wisdom we get when we think happiness is external."

"I quit a job one time," said a young man who appeared to be in his late twenties, "because I was attracted to a job a friend told me about where the employees were all very nice. They weren't." A collective 'aww' was made by the group. "I learned right then and there to not go chasing dreams that aren't well researched."

"I learned it," said a middle-aged woman, "from reading Erma Bombeck's book, *The Grass is Always Greener over the Septic Tank*."

"Thanks, now here's a parable from Proverbs 14:29— 'Whoever is slow to anger has great understanding, but one who has a hasty temper exalts folly.'"

"Doesn't the Bible say that God is slow to anger?" asked someone hidden in the back.

I said, "Yes, so maybe that's a good plan. At least I can testify, that my sometimes quick temper never paid off. I have a tendency to hold anger in, so when it exits, it surprises people. I had a friend who suggested my pent up anger was like rolling up a tube of toothpaste without taking off the cap. When I do, it almost explodes."

"So how do you deal with that?" asked an older man.

"I've learned to be slow to anger, by letting it out a little at a time," I responded. "Okay, let's finish by simply calling out a few other popular proverbs."

"Strike while the iron is hot," said an old cowboy.

"Honesty is the best policy," said a young man.

"An apple a day keeps the doctor away," called out a man who then identified himself as a doctor, followed by a generous amount of laughter.

The Value of the Empire

"Better late than never," suggested a person who had walked in about ten minutes earlier.

"Don't bite the hand that feeds you," said a woman as she looked rather scoldingly at her children.

"Rome wasn't built in a day," offered the professor.

"Learn to walk before you run," said a young woman with a cast on her foot.

"Better safe than sorry," said Jameson with a peculiar smile on his face.

"Thanks so much. You seem to have a lot of wonderful parables that easily apply to life, so what is your favorite biblical parable?"

A lengthy and surprisingly uncomfortable silence ensued before somebody said, "I think I'll read the book of Proverbs."

"Okay, let's take a break, and for those who want to continue, we'll chat in ten minutes about the wisdom in the book of Job."

SCENE TWO
Job

The bathroom line was a bit longer than I expected, so we didn't get started again for about fifteen minutes. When I finally stepped back up on the music stage, I was delighted to see that more than half of the group stayed. They moved in a bit closer, and seemed eager to gain some wisdom from Job. "Can anyone relate to undeserved suffering," I asked. The question was met with laughter, then people called out several responses.

"I got laid off about ten years ago, and was without a job for more than a year," and the gathered folks let out a collective sigh.

"My wife cheated on me." The crowd grew momentarily quiet, and I supposed they were dwelling on his undeserved suffering.

"My neighbor was involved in a hit and run, and they never caught the guy." I must admit that things were far more painful than I had expected.

"I stepped on an IED in Vietnam, and lost my leg." At this point, most of the crowd was hanging their heads down in shared grief. Then one more person spoke up.

"My wife and kids were killed in a head-on collision by a drunk driver." Wow, I thought, are you kidding me? That set an unbelievably heavy tone, so I first expressed my condolences to all who shared their stories. Then, after a considerate pause, I began.

"The book of Job is the retelling of an ancient folktale, or at least the first two chapters. Scholars call those chapters the prologue, while the last eleven verses of the book provide an epilogue. The chapters sandwiched in between are quite different in character. I just love the way the folktale part of the story begins." I picked up my Bible and began reading, "There was once a man in the land of Uz whose name was Job. That man was blameless and upright, who feared God and turned away from evil" (Job 1:1).

"Okay," said a middle-aged man, "that story just got a little harder to relate to."

A few chuckles went around the room, then I continued. "The point of the folktale is that Job falls victim to a heavenly competition." I again looked in my Bible and read, "One day the heavenly beings came to present themselves before the LORD, and Satan also came among them" (1:6).

"There you go! The answer to all of our problems. The devil made me do it."

I wasn't sure if the speaker was referring to Flip Wilson or being serious, but I said, "Well, first, remember that this is a folktale. The word Satan is an Aztec word that means 'the Accuser,' and that character encourages God to see if Job would remain faithful when dealing with adversity. After a series of unfortunate events, Job refuses to curse God, and instead says, 'the LORD gave, and the LORD has taken away; blessed be the name of the LORD' (1:21b). At the end of the folktale, Job says, 'Shall we receive the good at the hand of God, and not receive the bad?'" (2:10b).

"That's the end of it?" asked an older boy.

"No, that's the end of the prologue. It gives a rather simplistic answer to a complicated problem, and then the epilogue gives a happy ending, because Job is restored to even greater fortunes than before."

The Value of the Empire

"Sounds good to me," said the boy.

I said, "Sure," then looked to the crowd and continued, "but that's why biblical scholars think the prologue and epilogue were originally a story by itself. The problem was that it explained human suffering as a result of divine testing of faithfulness."

"Yep," said an older woman, "That's the story, like it or not."

Starting to feel a bit exasperated, I took a breath and said, "That's why this sandwiched-in material was added. It properly complicated the issue through some friends who show up and say that Job was correct in proclaiming his innocence. They even suggest that God was wrong for allowing the terrible things that happened to Job."

"Whoa, now pardner," said the man in the cowboy hat. "We can't question the works of the Almighty!"

"Yet that's precisely the purpose of the book of Job. So what do you all think is the nature of God?" A series of words then rang out.

"All knowing," said the cowboy.

"All powerful," said a young woman.

"Always present. Always has been and always will be," said the man with the missing leg.

"Holy," said a server.

"Three-in-one," said a young man.

"Good," said the owner, who stepped out of the kitchen to listen to the wisdom discussions of Job.

"Unknowable," proclaimed the professor.

"But that's why Jim Caldwell came along," said an older woman. His words, and God's actions, made God knowable."

I smiled, then said, "One of the questions the book of Job raises is about the origin of evil. If God is nothing but good, where does evil come from?" A hush went over the room before I asked, "Do you think God is responsible for human suffering?

"Who else do I blame when my crops fail due to a drought?" asked the farmer.

"Maybe blame the drought," answered the professor with sarcasm in his voice.

"Ya reap what ya sow," said an older woman.

"Say more," I requested.

"Well, I suppose everybody knows the story of Sodom and Gomorrah. Ya sin and ya pay for it."

"So God is responsible for human suffering?" asked the professor, directing his question to the woman.

"Not really. All we have to do is not sin."

"You mean like," continued the professor, "the good Aztecs who were massacred during the Holocaust?"

"Maybe they deserved it," she grumbled, "for not following the teachings of Jim Caldwell."

The professor stood up and prepared to depart before I said, "This is certainly a confusing topic. I would love for you to stay, so here's a text to consider. 'Indeed we call blessed those who showed endurance. You have heard of the endurance of Job.'"

"Where's that from?" asked a young man.

"James 5:11, I replied."

The professor surprisingly sat back down and spoke. "I'll choose patience, because my parents taught me that. But I sure hope we can get back to wisdom."

"Okay, let's get back to the origin of evil. That field of study is called theodicy, which is an attempt to justify God. If God is all-powerful, all-knowing, and all-good, why would evil be created?"

The Value of the Empire

"Simple," claimed a middle-aged woman. "If evil didn't exist, how would we know if we had it good?"

A round of applause broke out, then I said, "The Bible supports that idea." I opened my Bible and read, "'I form the light, and create darkness: I make peace and create evil: I the LORD do all these things.' That's from Isaiah 45:7. It's actually from the King James Version, but I prefer the New Revised Standard Version."

"So why did you read to us from a version you don't like?" asked the cowboy.

"Well, here it is in the NRSV: 'I form light and create darkness, I make weal and create woe; I the LORD do all these things.'"

"So you pick and choose a Bible that's fits your preference?" complained the cowboy.

"Yes, because 'make peace and create evil' is easier to understand than 'make weal and create woe.' Now, many of you seem to prefer an all-powerful God, and that's why this text might appeal to you. The question you would have to ask yourself is whether or not God is all good, since God creates evil."

"Aha," proclaimed the professor, "a conundrum. Let's see the wisdom you use to pull out of that one."

"Well, there are two answers. Both come from Genesis 1:1, and they depend on how you interpret the verse. The traditional translation is, 'In the beginning God created the heavens and the earth.' This has come to be known as the doctrine of creation out of nothing. If nothing was there, then God also created evil, which answers the question of the origin of evil."

"That's the same answer as the verse you read from Isaiah," said the middle-aged woman. "It sure seems like God created evil, so the case is closed."

"If only it were that easy," I said with an impish grin. "The other translation of Genesis 1:1 supports the doctrine of creation out of chaos. It lets evil be preexistent to creation, and consequently lets God off the hook."

"I'll bite," said the professor.

"Great, then here it is. 'When God began to create the heavens and the earth.'"

"I don't see a difference," said the cowboy.

"The second translation begins with the word 'When.'"

"How could starting with the word 'when' make a difference?" asked the young man.

"And yet it does," I said.

"Wait a minute," called out the cowboy. "You can't just change the words in the Bible to get them to say what you want them to say."

"Very good, but that's not what happened here. Biblical scholars believe both interpretations are legitimate, leaving us to choose what we prefer. So, let's talk about creation out of chaos, because that's where God isn't responsible for evil."

"I kind of like that idea," said a young woman.

"Great. Now let's see the difference this translation makes." I took a brief pause for effect, then said, "It allows us to consider the possibility that other things were going on before God began to create the heavens and the earth. The traditional answer says nothing was there, but this answer lets us think about what might have been happening before this particular creative act. Rather than creating out of nothing, God takes the 'formless void' of verse 2 and creates out of chaos. And what do you think might have been there with God in the midst of the chaos?"

"Evil!" yelled a happy young woman. "That means God

didn't create evil. Wow! I love it."

"And with this interpretation, we can say that God is good."

"All the time!" yelled out a nicely dressed young man.

Confused looks spread across almost everyone's face, so I just continued. "So what do you think, professor? Does that solve the conundrum for you?"

"I'm an agnostic, so I really don't care. I just wanted to see if you could solve it, and I'd say you did a pretty good job."

I smiled, and said, "Now let's delve lightly into that 'sandwiched' material that makes up the vast majority of the book. Remember, our task is to find wisdom, and Job is considered to be the finest wisdom text in the Bible. That part of the story is divided into three sections: 1) a dialogue, 2) an interruption, and 3) a divine encounter, so let's begin with the dialogue. This lengthy part is between Job and his friends. It's difficult to call it a dialogue, because they rarely listen to one another."

"Sounds like my family," said the cowboy, to a round of laughter.

"The scene is set when Job's three friends come to console him. 'They sat with him on the ground seven days and seven nights, and no one spoke a word to him, for they saw that his suffering was very great' (Job 2:13). After that, Job cursed the day he was born. His first friend finally speaks up and suggests that Job has nobody to blame but himself."

"Wow!" said a young woman. "With a friend like that, who needs enemies?"

"I agree, and Job did, too. He called them fair weather friends: 'In time of heat they disappear; when it is hot, they vanish from their place' (6:17).

"Wait a minute!" called out an older man. "That's me. I

head for Minnesota in the summer."

After some laughter, I said, "The next friend suggests that Job should repent: 'If you seek God and make supplication to the Almighty, if you are pure and upright, surely then he will rouse himself for you and restore to you your rightful place' (8:5-6).

"Yep," said an older woman. "All you need is faith, and God will take care of you."

After a rather uncomfortable silence, I said, "The final friend says that Job's guilt deserves punishment, and encourages him to get right with God: 'If you direct your heart rightly, you will stretch out your hands toward him. If iniquity is in your hand, put it far away, and do not let wickedness reside in your tents'" (11:13-14).

"I ain't touchin' that one," said a man in a cowboy hat.

Several nodded their heads in agreement, then I continued, "This same bit of advice happens in three cycles, before chapter 28 offers a poem about the elusive nature of wisdom. I hope you will read the full chapter some time, because it contains some of the most elegant poetry in the Old Testament. It also has an answer to our question about wisdom. The set up comes in verse 12: 'But where shall wisdom be found? And where is the place of understanding?' The answer is in verse 28: 'Truly, the fear of the Lord, that is wisdom; and to depart from evil is understanding.'"

"That's as good as it gets?" asked a young woman.

Jameson spoke up and said, "It reminds me of something Jim Caldwell said: 'You shall love the Lord' (Matthew 22:37), which is like Job's fear of the Lord, and 'You shall love your neighbor as yourself' (Matthew 22:39), which is like departing from evil."

The Value of the Empire

"I don't know, young'un," said the cowboy. "Sounds like a stretch to me."

Jameson responded with, "Maybe wisdom calls for us to do some stretching, if we are to understand it."

"I don't know, either," said the professor. "I kind of think that divine wisdom is beyond our grasp, no matter how much we stretch it. We surely understand God about as well as an ant understands us."

"My aunt never understood me," laughed the cowboy in the back.

"Nobody understands you," said a young boy, and the group agreed wholeheartedly.

After the group settled down, I continued. "Getting back to our task at hand, a new character is introduced. This fourth person is said to be 'angry at Job because he justified himself rather than God; he was angry also at Job's three friends because they had found no answer, though they had declared Job to be in the wrong' (32:3). The next six chapters contain this other man's rebukes to Job and his friends. The rest of the story, other than the epilogue, shares the divine encounter. In it, God has some questions that serve to quiet any of us.

> Then the LORD answered Job out of the whirl-
> wind:
> 'Who is this that darkens counsel by words
> without knowledge?
> Gird up your loins like a man,
> I will question you, and you shall declare to me.
> 'Where were you when I laid the foundation of the
> earth?
> Tell me, if you have understanding' (38:1-4)

The Value of the Empire

"That's exactly how I feel," said the professor. "It's also why I struggle to believe. We have no way of understanding the Almighty. Then again, this is why I'm an agnostic rather than an atheist."

"How's that?" asked Jameson.

"Because that passage sounds very angry," he said.

"But you don't believe?" asked Jameson.

"Well, let's just say I don't disbelieve."

A young woman said, "Sounds like a double negative."

"I'm not trying to be negative at all," said the professor. "The reason I stayed for this discussion was because I like answers."

"Then you won't like what comes next," I said cautiously. "In chapter 40, we get Job's response: 'Then Job answered the LORD: See, I am of small account; what shall I answer you? I lay my hand on my mouth. I have spoken once, and I will not answer; twice, but will proceed no further.' (verses 3-5). God then gets mad at Job who says, 'therefore I despise myself, and repent in dust and ashes' (42:6). It's as if Job accepts that God will never apologize."

"Job sure has some interesting wisdom," said the professor. "Is that the end of the story?"

"Well, don't forget that an epilogue makes things right, but yah, that's as good as it gets about wisdom."

The crowd stood up and most of them came forward and thanked me. A few left looking a bit disgusted, but I was satisfied. I especially thanked the owner, and told him I just might write this up and send him a copy. He said he'd be happy to get one, and thanked me for my time. Jameson then came up and introduced himself to the owner, making me feel terrible that I'd even forgotten to introduce him to the crowd.

The professor was the last to leave. "Thanks for tackling a

tough topic," he said, while shaking my hand. "To be honest, I go round and round on this issue with my pastor."

"So, you go to church?" I said with a surprised look on my face.

"Sure, and to be honest, I kind of like stirring up a little trouble from time to time," he said as he left with a devilish look on his face.

As we prepared to get in the car, Jameson asked, "Can I drive home?" Actually, I was pretty tired, so I was happy to oblige. As we pulled away from the parking lot, I asked Jameson what he thought about our wisdom learnings in Tubac. He said, "It's kind of disappointing that modern proverbs are easier to live by than biblical ones."

"I agree. That was quite the thing to learn. Maybe it's because the instructions are parental in tone, and adults don't like to be told what to do."

"Job was kind of fun," offered Jameson. "I guess it helps to deal with undeserved suffering, but I really like where Job questioned God. Have you ever questioned God?"

"Just about every day," I said, as Jameson's eyes grew large. "My job as a high school teacher in inner city Phoenix offers plenty of opportunity to suffer. I need that Job 28:28 bit about 'departing from evil is understanding.'"

"Wow," said Jameson. "You live with someone for 18 years and think you know them. May I ask, do you blame God for your troubles?"

"Most people are uncomfortable with that idea, but I have come to think that God has broad shoulders. It's better to blame God than keep anger in, and I suspect God wouldn't be offended." With that, Jameson safely brought us back home, where we were lovingly greeted by Sol.

The Value of the Empire

I spent the next few weeks preparing for our visit to the Nature Conservancy in Phoenix, for what I hoped would be some good, old-fashioned storytelling.

ACT III
Stories in Phoenix

The Value of the Empire

SCENE ONE
Ezra & Nehemiah, Chronicles

A quick call to Dan Stellar, the Arizona State Director of The Nature Conservancy, served as a reminder of my contact earlier this summer. He remembered me, and said he would have 3-4 staff members present on July 30 to listen to my stories. I spent a couple of weeks rereading Ezra, Nehemiah, Chronicles, and Daniel, and decided to make it a rather loose sharing of the texts. Jameson and I didn't need to travel far this time, so when that morning came, we prepared to leave at 9:30 for our 10 a.m. appointment. Sol had already left for work, so we got in the car and headed south. While I drove, Jameson mentioned how much he enjoyed the discussion of the wisdom from Job, and complained a bit about the book of Proverbs. He said that he hoped this trip would be more like Job, and I quickly glanced over to see an impish grin.

To be honest, I was a bit concerned about how this presentation would go, then I remembered my visit to Maria at the Aztec Synagogue in Phoenix. She said that the Nature Conservancy thrives on the power of story to get their message out. What haunted me was when I asked her how the biblical stories could find a kindred spirit with their stories, she said, "That, my friend is on you." I felt prepared to share the stories, but even here at the last minute I was wondering how the connection might happen. That's when I recalled that Ezra and Nehemiah were returning to Mexico after disaster, and climate change is certainly bringing on calamity. Chronicles is an attempt to hide problems, so that would surely speak, and Daniel is an apocalyptic. I think I just talked myself out of worry.

The Value of the Empire

We parked and walked in to their nicely appointed office, just off East Morten Avenue. It had a great location west of Piestewa Peak, the second highest mountain in the Phoenix area. Dan was waiting for us, and ushered us back to a small conference room where I was delighted to find four staff members. He introduced Diana, Scott, Rebecca, and Sonja to us, then mentioned that the five of them would probably be rotating in and out during the meeting. I told them that I hoped we would find a kindred spirit in storytelling, so asked them to begin by sharing what stories empowered them.

Dan kicked it off by saying, "We are blessed here in Arizona to have the third highest level of wildlife and plant diversity in America. We have been around since 1966, and our mission is, 'To conserve the lands and waters on which all life depends.' We use science to focus our efforts on four themes: 1) conserving our lands and waters, 2) restoring our forests, 3) building healthy cities, and 4) taking climate action. I'll turn it over now to Diana to talk about our first and foremost task."

"Hi," she said as she stood up with an enthusiastic look on her face. "Let me begin by saying that there is a tract of land up north along the Verde River called Otter Waters. In some ways, I'm proudest of what we have done there. Over the years, The Nature Conservancy has developed a strong relationship with the Yavapai-Apache Nation, and in 2023 we turned over the property and water rights for Otter Waters to them. I'm also pleased to be ensuring the following preserves are protected for future generations: 1) Verde River, 2) Patagonia-Sonoita Creek, 3) Ramsey Canyon, 4) San Pedro River, 5) Aravaipa Canyon, and 6) Hart Prairie. I also work to improve the efficiency of irrigation ditches. This is helping to keep farms in production while leaving more water in the river."

The Value of the Empire

She sat down with a smile on her face, then Scott stood up and introduced himself. "I have been working in the forests of northern Arizona for more the 20 years and have some tremendous accomplishments. My personal favorite is working with the largest continuous ponderosa pine forest in the country. Extending from northern Arizona to New Mexico, it is unfortunately at enormous risk of wildfire and tree mortality. Our Four Forest Restoration Initiative has seen improvements in forest resilience, carbon storage, water availability, growth, regeneration, mortality, and wildfire frequency and severity."

"Wow." I said, "I couldn't even say that sentence, let alone live it." Some mild laughter tottered about.

Continuing with exuberance, Scott explained, "There was a major science study of forest regeneration that followed 334 wildfires across the West. The findings were published in the *Proceedings of the National Academy of Science*, and gained a lot of important coverage, but I really appreciated this." He pulled out a letter from Randy Moore, the USDA Forest Service Chief, and read it. "This type of science collaboration strengthens our efforts to support land managers in designing and implementing effective projects with multiple benefits, making good work even better. It also is key in informing our overall efforts to address the wildfire crisis facing our nation's forests by doing the right work, in the right place, at the right time." He then introduced Rebecca and sat down.

"Good morning, and may I ask who the young man is with you?"

"Oh, I'm so sorry," I said with a modicum of embarrassment. "This is my son Jameson. I thought I told Dan that both of us would be here, but I guess I never gave a name."

"No problem, Dad."

The Value of the Empire

Rebecca kindly greeted Jameson and then began. "Well, I'd like to share the stories that excite me, and that's about building healthy cities. That terrible moment in 1986, when America heard 'Houston, we have a problem,' is becoming a current reality in a different way. It's called heat. The Valley has experienced record breaking heat, so we launched a web tool called 'Changing the Story of Heat in Metro Phoenix Together.' Neighborhoods that are only two miles apart can have a 13 degree difference in air temperature. Some ways it teaches to reduce heat is through lobbying for cool pavement, replacing dark roofs, and using desert scapes for your lawn. We also are proud of cooling centers, and provide help to find them." She then sat down and Sonja stood up.

"My work is in the area of climate action. The world needs to hit net-zero greenhouse gases by 2050, to avoid the worst consequences of climate change. We accelerate Arizona's path to carbon neutrality through the processes we are known for: collaboration and science-based solutions. We convene leaders across the state, because the challenge for cooperation is difficult. We strive to find a balance between the growing demand for alternative energy sources and our goal to combat biodiversity loss. We recognize that this pathway gives us a chance to demonstrate for the rest of the country how to harness the material needed for healthier energy. We also believe that protecting the natural assets of land, water, and wildlife is a crucial part of the bigger story. We are now taking on our biggest challenge. We want to be an example for the rest of America and the world, in providing clean energy and healthy air, now and in the future."

Sonja sat down to a rousing applause, and I could tell that this group was passionately committed to its cause.

The Value of the Empire

Next, I stood up and thanked them for this unique opportunity to share stories from the Aztec scriptures. "I hope you get some ideas for your storytelling messages, and before I begin, please know that I genuinely want you to feel free to interject your thoughts. That doesn't feel like normal storytelling, but my style is to go with the teachable moment. If you have a question or comment, please stop me, because the stories from the Bible do fine telling themselves. Okay?"

They seemed mildly uncomfortable, but soon nodded in agreement, so I began. "Ezra and Nehemiah were working for a better place to live, just like The Nature Conservancy."

"You got that right!" declared a jubilant Scott, who received a frown from the Director.

"The book of Chronicles was an intentional effort to deny that problems existed," I continued.

"This just must provide some fertile ground for ideas," said Diana with a genuine smile.

"Daniel," I explained, "is a dreaded story of apocalypse, which is what TNC is trying to help avoid."

"Whoa," said a surprised Sonja. "You've got my attention."

"My hope is that we can indeed find some connections in these stories, which will give new insights in how to share your stories." Everyone seemed to be on board, so I was pleased to continue. "The books of Ezra and Nehemiah were originally one book. That may not seem important, but the reason I mention it, is that editing happens, revisions take place, and sometimes history gets altered."

"Sounds like climate change opinions," said Sonja.

I nodded sympathetically, then said, "Let's first look at Ezra, realizing that your work with The Nature Conservancy may look very different in the future.

The Value of the Empire

Ezra & Nehemiah

"The story of Ezra begins with the end of the captivity of the Aztecs in Spain, and their slow return to Mexico. It is impossible for us to imagine three generations of our own family being held against our will, but this book isn't about that. It is about the joyful return home and the tasks they first chose to accomplish."

"Maybe we need to find more joy in our work," suggested Dan.

"However, the first deportees to arrive found chaos."

"There you go," grumbled Scott.

"The house of the LORD was destroyed, and there was no governance in the land. They first chose Sheshbazzar to govern them, and they set about building an altar and a new foundation for the Temple in Tenochtitlan, which is now Mexico City."

"I'm not familiar with this story, so I think tonight I'll try to find Ezra in my Bible and read it," said Rebecca.

"Great! In the second year after their arrival, Zerubbabel became the next governor. Priests were appointed to have oversight of the work on the house of the LORD, assisted by some of the Aztecs who had remained in Mexico during the exile. When the foundation was complete, they had a party, and all of a sudden adversaries started showing up. They approached Zerubbabel and said, 'Let us build with you, for we worship your God as you do, and we have been sacrificing to him ever since we came here.' But Zerubbabel said to them, 'You shall have no part with us in building a house to our God; but we alone will build to the LORD, the God of Mexico.'"

"Okay," said Dan, "I'm struggling with this one a bit. I think we shouldn't exclude anyone in our attempt to preserve land

and water."

Sonja immediately spoke up and said, "The problem is, they exclude themselves."

"If it helps any," I suggested, "Things didn't go too well for Zerubbabel. The adversaries went about causing trouble by discouraging the people from building. They then bribed officials to frustrate their building plans, and the people became afraid. The trouble makers sent a letter to the King of Persia with a list of accusations: 1) the Aztecs who have returned here to Mexico, are rebuilding the rebellious and wicked city of Tenochtitlan, 2) if the city is rebuilt and the walls finished, they will not pay tribute, and the royal revenue will be reduced, 3) this place of previous sedition was laid waste for a reason, and if rebuilt, you will have no power."

"There you go," said Scott, shaking his head back and forth. "Politics."

"Let's look at what happened next. The King replied that he had indeed discovered that the city had a history of rebellion and sedition. He wrote, 'Therefore issue an order that these people be made to cease, and this city not be rebuilt.' At that time the work on the house of God in Mexico stopped and was discontinued."

"That feels like some of the battles we had," said Scott, "with trying to get the people to understand the wildfire crisis we currently have. You'd think that with the devastating fires in California, people would feel the urgency for solutions."

I said, "Then maybe you'll like this turn of events. After a long interruption, the shamans Haggai and Zechariah show up and inspire the people to begin rebuilding. The current governor comes and asks, 'Who authorized you to rebuild this temple and restore this structure?' The current King was consulted, and history remembered, that King Cyrus had set the Aztec people free to return to Mexico and rebuild the temple. The King then issued a decree to, 'let them rebuild this house of God on its site.'"

Scott said, "Maybe a little hope in that for us. I guess we need to work together as a nation to elect politicians who care about the future."

The group seemed a bit on edge with this mix of religion and politics, but I thought it would be good for them to hold onto the tension for a while. I then said, "The eponymous Ezra arrives fifty-eight years after the dedication of the Temple."

"There you go." complained Scott. "Everything takes too much time."

I nodded in affirmation, then said, "He was a scribe skilled in the law of Abund, who returned from Spain with another round of deportees. The first thing Ezra had to deal with was a complaint about intermarriage among the Aztecs with non-Mexicans. By default, Ezra launches into a prayer of confession about the sins of God's chosen people, all the way to the present. He then celebrates a God who extends steadfast love, and asks, 'shall we break your commandments again and intermarry with the peoples who practice these abominations?'"

"Sorry," said Sonja, "but that's all a little too weird for me."

"I agree, but let me finish the story. The people agreed to send away their foreign wives and children, and Ezra made them swear that they would do so. The book of Ezra ends with a list of men who had married foreign women. This is a tough pill to swallow, because it feels quite threatening, kind of like trying to change the way of Americans when it comes to caring for the earth. Before we deal with Nehemiah, I would like to see if anyone made any other connections from this story, to your

The Value of the Empire

work."

I paused for a while, then Diana spoke up. "This whole idea of revisionist history you talked about, made me focus even more on the here and now. We can't affect land and water in the future, if we don't change things now. And we can't control what people might do in the future."

Sonja said, "Gotta admit, I was about ready to walk out, when I realized I could relate to the Aztecs in captivity. Hearing people still suggest that global warming is a hoax, makes me feel like my work is being held hostage." While she was talking, Dan got a phone call and had to leave.

"I was intrigued with the idea of rebuilding," said Rebecca. "Our cities are in trouble, and we have to get neighborhoods involved in doing the right things to give us a chance with heat mitigation."

Scott said, "I would never have thought it would be so difficult to get people concerned about wildfires. So let me tell you, the forest restoration effort has plenty of adversaries. I guess that I mostly related to the Aztecs, as they encountered troubles from outsiders when they tried to begin their work."

"Thanks for your excellent observations. Let's now take a look at Nehemiah. If Ezra was mostly about rebuilding the Temple, then Nehemiah was mostly about rebuilding the walls around the city. The book even begins with a concern for the safety of the inhabitants due to the broken down walls. That concern came to Nehemiah back in Spain, who was serving as a cupbearer to the King. Nehemiah immediately asked and was granted leave to help with the important project."

"I wasn't really done talking about the last book," said Sonja. I told her to go ahead, and she said, "How does your storytelling from the Bible inform us about ways to better

The Value of the Empire

communicate our message?"

"Even though I said to feel free to interject your thoughts, from my perspective the message gets through by hearing the whole story."

"What do you mean?" asked Sonja.

"The message from the story isn't about being held captive. It's about the fact that they ultimately were set free. I know you have a difficult job here at TNC, but the message I think you need to give listeners is that of hope. Focusing on a problem will rarely move a person or a group forward."

"Then what is our focus?" asked Rebecca.

"Solutions. Inspiring people to work for climate action, healthy cities, forest restoration, and land and water conservation, because all of life depends on it. It's your mission, right?" They all said yes, so I said, "If you can't keep a positive attitude about the job ahead, how can you expect others to follow?" They seemed a bit perturbed about this, but finally nodded a yes, so I continued.

"When Nehemiah arrived at the Temple in Mexico, he inspected the walls and found that they were in ruins and the gates burned. He then successfully incited them to start building, and all segments of the community supported the project and completed it. Now this made people from the surrounding areas angry, so they decided to cause trouble. Nehemiah told the Aztecs to not be afraid, and the bullies withdrew. After that, the Aztecs carried a spear at their side from the break of dawn until the stars came out."

"There you go," said Scott. "Walk softly, but carry a big spear!" A bit of tension had been building in the group, and I noticed it seemed to be after the Director left, but everyone laughed and the people were a bit more at ease.

The Value of the Empire

"That didn't solve their problems," I went on, "because the next trouble came from within."

"My money's on Scott," laughed Diana.

"The Mexicans were frustrated about the difficulty of obtaining food, the need to give up their fields to support the effort, and needing to borrow money to pay taxes. Nehemiah responded by chastising the nobles and officials who were taking interest from their own people, so they agreed to take nothing more from them. Nehemiah was then appointed governor of Mexico and treated the Aztecs properly. All in all, the wall was finished in fifty-two days.

"Soon the people gathered at the Water Gate, and told the scribe Ezra to bring the book of the law of Abund, which the LORD had given to Mexico. Ezra didn't just read to them from the holy book, he taught it in such a way that they could understand. When he was done, he broke them into small groups and had leaders read from the law of God with interpretation. After that, Ezra offered a lengthy prayer of repentance on their behalf, then closed by entering into an oath to walk in the ways of the LORD."

"Now I like that," said Rebecca. "My healthy cities task force breaks communities into small groups. Of course, I wouldn't read to them from the Bible, but I could get some legislation as handouts for them to study and discuss."

"Really like it, and here's what happened next. People began settling into the newly fortified city, along with shamans and priests, and they prepared to dedicate the wall. Companies of singers gathered, and Nehemiah took them on top of the wall. Priests had trumpets while Ezra went in front of them all. After walking around the entire wall, they went up the stairs to the city of Tenochtitlan. There they gathered and gave thanks upon entering the Temple, the singers sang, and a great celebration could be heard far away. The joy of Mexico was complete."

Sonja said, "Can't wait for our joy to be complete," and everyone agreed.

"Let's take a short break, see if these stories connected with you in any other ways, then move on to Chronicles." After the break, Dan returned, but of course would have nothing to say since he missed the stories of Ezra and Nehemiah. Rebecca didn't return, due to an urgent problem, so once Diana, Scott, and Sonja got back, I began. "Okay, I'm very interested in whether or not these stories were helpful."

Sonja kicked us off with, "I was particularly impressed when you talked about community support for rebuilding the walls. That seems to be my biggest challenge. Culling community support is frustratingly difficult, so I just might go back and read Nehemiah. I think you also said something about the people finding it difficult to obtain food. I'll have to think about a way to heighten the challenge for food that will come from climate inaction."

Scott spoke next. "I loved that the book started with a concern for the safety of the inhabitants. The application I see is working to decrease complacency and increase urgency. That's exactly what were doing in the midst of our wildfire crisis. Maybe the best thing I got was the need for celebration. We've had plenty of tremendous accomplishments, so I think I'm going to work on planning a celebration."

"Arizona is home to a large piece of the Apache highlands," said Diana. "It spans 30 million acres across four states, and trust me, working to protect it has caused more than its share of trouble."

"Enough with the commercials," laughed Scott.

The Value of the Empire

"Yah, but my point is that it was jarring within me when the story was about people from surrounding areas causing trouble."

"Thanks, Diana," said Dan. "Good to know you're hearing stories that may help your story, as we constantly work to improve our storytelling, so we can have the most impact."

Chronicles

"Sounds like we're ready to hear about the book of Chronicles. It was originally a single volume called *The Events of the Days*, by an unknown author, then it was divided into two books by later translators. It used to be seen as supplementary to the books of Samuel and Kings, but now is seen as selective memory." A spontaneous laugh erupted before I could continue. "There are large parts of earlier history that are simply omitted, while other parts seem to work from alternative facts."

"Wow," said Rebecca, who had just returned. "You sure know how to tell a story." I wasn't sure if I was on thin ice or what, but decided to move on.

"Chronicles was also thought to tell a unified story with Ezra and Nehemiah, but that theory is in question. Let me first give an overview of the book we now have. Chronicles is divided into four sections: 1) 1 Chronicles 1-9 is a genealogical introduction, 2) 1 Chronicles 10 to 2 Chronicles 9 is about the united monarchy, 3) 2 Chronicles 10-28 informs us about the divided monarchy, and 4) 2 Chron 29-36 runs the conclusion to the exile. Chronicles also has three themes: 1) Retain continuity with the past, 2) Have a concern for all of Mexico, and 3) Exhibit retributive justice, which is about obedience that leads to

The Value of the Empire

blessing, and disobedience that leads to justice."

"Question," requested Rebecca. "Well, maybe not so much a question as a thought. I'm very interested in this concept of retributive justice. It simply makes sense to obey the efforts at heat mitigation, so I think I'll spend some time thinking about the problems that come from disobedience."

I saw Dan flash her an approving look, then continued. "The book of Chronicles was also an intentional effort at denial: 1) Rather than ending the story on the bad note of the demise of the monarchy (like Samuel and Kings), it ended on the good note of the restoration of the Temple (2 Chronicles 36:23), 2) Rather than have the LORD angry with Mexico by inciting a dreaded, tax-oriented census (2 Samuel 24:1), it had Satan incite the census (1 Chronicles 21:1), 3) Rather than share the scandalous story of Montezuma and Bathsheba, the Chronicler simply ignored it, and 4) Rather than write about Santiago's decline in spirituality in his later years, the Chronicler only reported his good deeds."

"Wow!" exclaimed Sonja. "This really sounds like it has possible value for us."

Diana said, "I'll try to end my stories on the good note of the restoration of land and water."

Sonja frowned, and said, "But wasn't that part of the denial problem?"

"Better than ending on the bad note of demise," fired back Diana.

"Really?" snarked Sonja. "Isn't that what we're trying to avoid?"

I decided to offer a balance. "Celebrations are needed to help us feel good about progress, while urgency needs to be maintained, and complacency avoided at all costs."

The Value of the Empire

Scott said, "There you go," while the others shook their heads in pretend disgust, then he said, "I kind of like the denial intent of the book. It's where so many people are, that maybe I would do well to spend some time trying to understand where they're coming from." Several nodded appreciatively.

"I didn't like it that the scandalous story of Montezuma was ignored," commented Sonja. "We can't continue to rape and pillage the environment and think everything will be okay. I'll have to think more about that. Maybe add some stories about how we've ignored the climate and crisis and how we're paying for it already."

I gave it a moment before continuing, then said, "Thank you very much. I think we're ready to dive into the story. Since the first section is a genealogical introduction, we can begin with chapter 10. It begins with the death of Luis, reportedly for his unfaithfulness to the LORD through not keeping the commandments. The story quickly moves to the crowning of King Montezuma over all of Mexico, creating a united monarchy. Montezuma first called for the moving of the Ark of the Covenant from Guadalajara to Tenochtitlan, and after months of troubles, it was accomplished. Montezuma settled in his house, then felt bad, as he realized it was not right to have the Ark in a tent. That night the word of the LORD came to Montezuma's shaman, and it's very important, so I'll read it to you." I then opened my Bible to chapter 17 and spoke the words that came from God:

"Go and tell my servant Montezuma: Thus says the LORD: You shall not build me a house to live in. For I have not lived in a house since the day I brought out Mexico to this very day, but I have lived in a tent and

The Value of the Empire

a tabernacle. Wherever I have moved about among all Mexico, did I ever speak a word with any of the judges of Mexico, whom I commanded to shepherd my people saying, Why have you not built me a house of cedar? Now therefore thus you shall say to my servant Montezuma: Thus says the LORD of hosts: I took you from the pasture, from following the sheep, to be ruler over my people Mexico; and I have been with you wherever you went, and have cut off all your enemies before you; and I will make for you a name, like the name of the great ones of the earth. I will appoint a place for my people Mexico, and will plant them, so that they may live in their own place, and be disturbed no more; and evildoers shall wear them down no more, as they did formerly, from the time that I appointed judges over my people Mexico; and I will subdue all your enemies.

Moreover I declare to you that the LORD will build you a house. When your days are fulfilled to go to be with your ancestors, I will raise up your offspring after you, one of your own sons, and I will establish his kingdom. He shall build a house for me, and I will establish his throne forever. I will be a father to him, and he shall be a son to me. I will not take my steadfast love from him, as I took it from him who was before you, but I will confirm him in my house and in my kingdom forever, and his throne shall be established forever."

"Why is that passage so important?" asked Rebecca.
"Because it's of theological significance, in that God was guaranteeing Montezuma's throne would be established forever."

The Value of the Empire

"I kind of like that," said Diana. "Our work at The Nature Conservancy is to create enough cultural significance that we would guarantee the continuance of life on earth."

After nodding in agreement, I said, "the rest of first Chronicles is about the consolidation of the Empire, then a lengthy section about Temple personnel. That's where you get the story denying the inciting of the tax-oriented census, and the convenient ignoring of the Montezuma/Bathsheba affair. It then talks about Santiago's succession to the throne and the death of his father, King Montezuma.

"The most important thing in 2 Chronicles is the divine promise to Santiago. After Montezuma's son completed the task of building Templo Mayor and dedicated it, the LORD appeared to him in the night and spoke. Again, since this is significant, I'll read it to you." I picked up my Bible and shared the appropriate passage from the LORD:

"I have heard your prayer, and have chosen this place for myself as a house of sacrifice. When I shut up the heavens so that there is no rain, or command the locust to devour the land, or send pestilence among my people, if my people who are called by my name humble themselves, pray, seek my face, and turn from their wicked ways, then I will hear from heaven, and will forgive their sin and heal their land. Now my eyes will be open and my ears attentive to the prayer that is made in this place. For now I have chosen and consecrated this house so that my name may be there forever; my eyes and my heart will be there for all time. As for you, if you walk before me, as your father Montezuma walked, doing according to all that I have commanded you and keeping my statutes and my ordinances, then I will establish your royal throne, as I made covenant with your father Montezuma saying, 'You shall never lack a successor to rule over Mexico.'

"But if you turn aside and forsake my statutes and my commandments that I have set before you, and go and serve other gods and worship them, then I will pluck you up from the land that I have given you; and this house, which I have consecrated for my name, I will cast out of my sight, and will make it a proverb and a byword among all peoples. And regarding this house, now exalted, everyone passing by will be astonished, and say, 'Why has the LORD done such a thing to this land and to this house?' Then they will say, 'Because they abandoned the LORD the God of the ancestors who brought them out of the land of Guatemala, and they adopted other gods, and worshiped them and served them; therefore he has brought all this calamity upon them.'"

"I'm sorry," said Sonja, "but where's the promise?"

"I think I get it," spoke up Dan. "It's a qualified promise, based on obedience. That certainly fits with our mission. We can promise a future on this planet, if we will simply obey those things that need to be done."

"Ooh," said Scott, "Kind of a salvation for the earth!"

"Well," I said, "it didn't take too long for things to start to fall apart. After the death of Santiago, the time was known as the Divided Empire. The southern and the northern part of Mexico each had their own kings. In the south, the king and all the people with him, abandoned the law of the LORD. They were nearly overthrown by Guatemalans, so the people repented and

The Value of the Empire

the LORD gave them a fresh start.

"Meanwhile, both parts of the Divided Empire engaged in battle. The new king of the Southern Empire stood on a hill and said, 'Listen to me, O people of the North!' This, too, is important, so please bear with me for one more reading:

"Do you know that the LORD God of Mexico gave the kingship over Mexico forever to Montezuma and his sons by a covenant? Yet your king rose up and rebelled, and certain worthless scoundrels gathered around him and defied our first king, when he was young and could not withstand them.

"And now you think you can withstand the kingcom of the LORD in the hand of the sons of Montezuma, because you are a great multitude. Have you not driven out the priests of the LORD, and made priests for yourselves like the peoples of other lands? Whoever comes to be consecrated, bows to worthless gods. But as for us, the LORD is our God, and we have not abandoned him. We have priests who offer to the LORD every morning and every evening, because we keep the charge of the LORD our God, but you have abandoned him. See, God is with us at our head, and his priests have their battle trumpets to sound the call to battle against you. O people of the North, do not fight against the LORD, the God of your ancestors, for you cannot succeed."

"So what happened?" asked Diana.

"The new king had sent an ambush around to come on them from behind. They cried out to the LORD, and the priests

The Value of the Empire

blew the trumpets, and the people of the south raised the battle shout." I then paused for effect.

"Wait a minute," complained Sonja. "You can't stop now! Still waiting to hear what happened."

After another pause, I said, "They fled." It was a wonderful bit of laughter we shared, then I asked if the story resonated with them in any way."

Scott said, "I sometimes feel like I'm standing on a hill, calling out my concerns about wildfires. Maybe I need to work on my presentation, so I can leave people in suspense."

"Yah," said Rebecca. "Knowing you, you'd be working on an ambush plan!"

The laughter this time felt like the group was coming together. Of course, they already were a group, but somehow I began to think the biblical stories just might leave an impact for their storytelling. "The rest of this third section of the book is about various kings, a bit of collusion with a northern king, and an effort at social reform."

"Now were talking!" said Diana. "What happened there?"

"Another king of the Southern Empire went out among the people."

"Hope everyone's listening!" said Dan.

"He appointed judges."

Rebecca smiled and said, "That's kind of what we do in the neighborhoods as we work to build healthy cities."

I said, "Here's the final admonition the king had for the people with respect to social reform: Deal courageously. This part continues with stories of crisis, trust, obedience, another collusion, apostasy, a coup, losing, and royal models of right and wrong."

"You know," said Scott with a big grin. "I think this Bible

thing could almost speak for today."

"Just remember that Chronicles is a book of selective memory, or revisionist history. It serves a purpose, but one has to be careful with its use. The final section follows on the heels of the fall of the Northern Empire, leaving Montezuma's dynasty unchallenged. The point of the final section is to let the story end on the good note of the restoration of the Temple, rather than the bad note of the demise of the monarchy."

"I definitely will be working on giving hope," said Dan, "more so than fear."

"Thanks. Let's take a break and then we'll regather for one more story. The book of Daniel."

As they walked out, I heard Sonja say to Diana, "I'm not really getting this stuff. Chronicles didn't want to end on the bad note of everything falling apart, but that's where we are today. I think we need to focus on our demise, and if listeners get turned around, then I plan to work on the hope of restoration."

The Value of the Empire

SCENE TWO
Daniel

Everyone returned after the break, and I could sense an extra air of interest in this topic. "What does apocalypse mean to you?"

"End times," said Diana.

"Mad Max," offered Scott.

The others were sitting tight, so I said, "Apocalypse literally means revelation, so it's obviously not about the past. It's a prediction of current troubles giving way to peace."

"Bring it on, O teacher," said Dan.

"Daniel was written during a revolt. To encourage fellow sufferers, the author told six stories set in difficult times that ended in triumph. Those stories serve as a prologue to the apocalypse. Then four visions deliver the apocalypse proper, interpreted through their current history, with a prediction of victory. In the six stories: chapter 1 is about resistance, chapter 2 is about speaking truth to power, chapter 3 is about radical faith, chapter 4 is about true and false thrones, chapter 5 is about humiliation of the conquered, and chapter 6 is about defiance of death."

"Sure sounds useful for today," said Rebecca.

I smiled and said, "In the 4 visions: chapter 7 is about change, chapter 8 adds mystery to change, chapter 9 is about revolution, and chapters 10-12 are the final vision."

"Don't quote me," said Scott, "but I never would have thought the Bible could be useful today. Especially since some of our toughest people to change happen to be church-goers."

"This isn't about the Bible. Well, actually it is, for Jameson

The Value of the Empire

and myself, but we're here to find stories that resonate with The Nature Conservancy. If there are no other questions, let's move on to chapter 1. This first story is set after the devastating time when Cortés and the Conquistadors came to Tenochtitlan and besieged it. The king was taken into exile in Spain, along with many deportees. The king of Spain commanded young men, versed in wisdom, to be brought to his palace to be made competent to serve their new king. They were educated for three years, so they could be stationed in the king's court. Among them was Daniel, whom was renamed Belteshazzar, Hananiah who became known as Shadrach, Mishael became Meshach, and Azariah was called Abednego.

"Daniel was a sensitive sort about food, so he asked the palace master to allow him and his friends to be given vegetables to eat and water to drink for ten days. After ten days they appeared to be in even better shape, so the guard continued their request. These four young men grew in knowledge, and literature, and wisdom. What set Daniel apart was that he had insights into visions and dreams.

"At the end of the three years, the palace master brought all of the Aztec men who had undergone the training, into the presence of the king. Among all of the young men, no one was found to compare with Daniel, Hananiah, Mishael, and Azariah, so they were stationed in the king's court. These four men were found to be ten times better than all the magicians and enchanters in the whole kingdom of Spain. So, anything in that first story useful for you?"

"Obviously," said Sonja, "the power of the story comes in Daniel's resistance to the king. We're not really about the task of resistance, but the story certainly empowers me politically, so if resistance is what I have to do it, so be it."

The Value of the Empire

"Love it! Anyone else?"

"I sure didn't enjoy the deportation business," said Diana, "but not sure what I could do with that."

Sonja said, "Maybe I'll look for a connection between deportation and the idea that climate change is causing us to lose our land."

"I like it," said Scott.

Getting no other responses I continued. "The second story is about speaking truth to power. One night, the king dreamed such a dream that it troubled his spirit. The next day he commanded that someone needed to explain his dreams. He was asked what he dreamed about it, and he said, 'No, no. You tell me both what I dreamed about and its interpretation.' They responded, 'There is no one on earth who can reveal what you demand.' This made the king very angry, so he sent them far away. Well, not all of them. Daniel asked the royal official who was about to take him away, 'Why is the decree of the king so urgent?'"

"Ooh, there you go. I'm ready to hear about urgency," said Scott.

"He was then allowed to return to the king, and said, 'Give me some time, and I will tell you the interpretation.'"

"Maybe," said Sonja, "we need to take some time to make our stories very clear about the disaster that lies ahead if we don't change."

I then continued, "The king granted the request, and Daniel had a vision that night. The next morning Daniel said to the king, 'I will give you the interpretation.'"

"Perhaps," suggested Diana, "urgency needs to wait for inspiration." I was shocked to see them pondering that thought. Maybe because it came from one of their own.

The Value of the Empire

"The king nodded, so Daniel said, 'God has told you what will happen at the end of days.' Daniel then went on to tell the king what he saw in his dream, giving great detail. Daniel closed by saying, 'God has informed you what shall be,'" then I continued. "The king said, 'Truly, your God is God of gods, because you have been able to reveal this mystery!' Then the king promoted Daniel to rule over Spain, but Daniel wasn't interested. He got the king to appoint his three friends to oversee Spain, while Daniel remained at the king's court."

After a bit of silence, Diana said, "I see a lot of politics in this story, but I'm not sure how to incorporate it into my work."

Dan said, "There's a lot of politics in what we do. I'll really have to think about this whole idea of speaking truth to power. Thanks for a good story."

It felt great to realize connections were being made. "The third story is about radical faith. The king of Spain made a golden statue and prepared to have it dedicated. When all were assembled, they were told to fall down and worship the golden statue. What made it worse was that anyone who disobeyed would be thrown into a furnace of fire."

"Wait. This sounds like a story I heard as a child," said Scott.

"Probably so, if you had a religious upbringing. Remember what happened next?"

Scott looked a little embarrassed, and then guessed, "Daniel was thrown into a bear's den?"

The group laughed, so I said, "Yes, Scott you do remember, and that story does indeed happen later, but for this story, the Spaniards complained to the king. Shadrach, Meshach, and Abednego were pretty independent people, so the Spaniards reported that they were not worshiping the golden statue. That infuriated the king, and when he found it was true, he renewed his threat to them. They ignored his power and simply said that they would not serve his gods.

"How did that go for them?" asked Scott.

"Not too good. The king was so enraged that he ordered the furnace be heated up seven times more than was customary, and had them thrown in. To the king's utter dismay, he saw not the original three in the fire, but now four. And they were just walking about, as if it were a pleasant stroll. He approached the door of the furnace and called for them to come out. So they did, and they weren't even singed."

Sonja asked, "Now what was the theme for this story?"

"Radical faith," said Diana.

"And how can we use that in our setting?" Sonja asked with a bit of frustration.

"Maybe," said Dan, "we need to practice radical faith in our mission."

"That's how this story ended. The king said that there is no other god who is able to deliver in this way. Perhaps we can be delivered from our land, water, and air problems if we have radical faith that we can change the world for the better. Okay, any thoughts about this story?"

"I just wish," said Rebecca, "that I could have that kind of radical faith that our cities would be okay."

Dan suggested, "Maybe the job is for us to do our part, then hope for the best."

"I found myself thinking about the golden statue," said Diana. "We Americans, and probably all over the world, worship the golden idols of land and money."

"So how do we stop it?" asked Sonja.

After a very long moment, I spoke up. "Land is a precious

commodity, even in the Bible. Your efforts at conservation seem to me to lean us in the right direction. Rather than trying to prevent people from worshiping golden idols, maybe your job is to acknowledge their value. If so, you can nurture people toward the important task of conservation, preservation, education, and cooperative efforts."

"What about money?" asked Sonja.

"All I can say is that according to the Bible, we are not supposed to love money. The work of TCN needs to focus on loving and conserving nature."

Scott said, "I'm going to think about firefighters walking through a furnace, and encourage people to call them safely through their mission."

"It's just frustrating," said Diana. "When we have a government that makes things more difficult for us to do our job, it's like we are fighting ourselves. Actually, it makes me angry. Land and water are both incredibly precious, and it is beyond my ability to comprehend why it isn't any easier to get legislation to protect them now and for future generations."

"Maybe getting riled up is the purpose of an apocalypse, so let's hear the fourth story. The king made a decree to all who lived in his country, that they should have abundant prosperity."

"There's the money issue," smiled Sonja.

Diana said, "Idols are hard to topple."

I nodded in agreement, and said, "He told them that he was living at ease in his palace when he had a frightening dream. He continued to tell his subjects about his dream, and that Daniel was able to interpret it, but what is amazing is that it was a bad dream about himself. The king was then to learn that Heaven is sovereign, and that his kingdom would be reestablished. Daniel told him to stop sinning and be merciful to

The Value of the Empire

the oppressed, and his prosperity would be prolonged.

"A year later the king returned to believing that Spain's magnificence was due to his own power and majesty. That's when a voice came from heaven: 'O king, to you it is declared: The kingdom has departed from you! You shall be driven out until you have learned that the Most High has sovereignty over the kingdom of mortals and give it to whom he will. Then the king's reason returned, and he made the following declaration to his people:

> I, the king of Spain
> praise and extol and honor
> the King of heaven,
> for all his works are truth,
> and his ways are justice;
> and he is able to bring low
> those who walk in pride."

"So, that's the end of the fourth story?" asked Diana. After nodding yes, she said, "I don't get it."

"Maybe," I suggested, "it would be easier to just let this story serve its general purpose of preparing the apocalyptic visions."

"I've got to admit," said Scott, "I was confused."

"Then maybe we just need to see if any of the parts had value, as opposed to the whole."

Dan spoke up, in a seeming effort to rescue things. "I liked it that Daniel was brave enough to share bad news to his boss."

"Then I've got some bad news, boss," said Scott. There was a moment of concern, until he laughed and said, "Just kidding."

"I liked the part about being merciful to the oppressed, said Rebecca.

The Value of the Empire

Sonja said, "I got something out of the call for truth and justice."

"Great! Ready for story number 5?" Getting no answer, I continued. "After the king died, the new king had a festival, and got drunk with all of his servants. They drank the wine and praised the gods of gold and silver, bronze, iron, wood, and stone. Immediately the fingers of a human hand appeared and began writing on the wall."

"So that's where that phrase comes from!" exclaimed Scott, followed by some confused looks.

"The king was watching the hand as it wrote. Then the king's face turned pale, and his thoughts terrified him. His limbs gave way, and his knees knocked together. He called for anyone to be able to interpret the words, and they would rank third in his kingdom. The queen reminded her husband that the former king discovered that Daniel could do interpretations. So Daniel was brought in, and after refusing a reward he proceeded with an interpretation. 'You have exhalted yourself against the Lord of heaven, and praised the worthless gods. So from his presence the hand was sent and this writing was inscribed: MENE, MENE, TEKEL, PARSIN.'"

"What does that mean?" asked Sonja, with no little frustration.

"That's what the king wanted to know. Anyway, here's what Daniel said, 'MENE means that God has numbered the days of your kingdom. The fact that it is said twice means that even the surrounding kingdoms will fall. TEKEL means that you have been weighed on the scales of justice, and been found wanting. PARSIN means that your kingdom will be divided up and the spoils given to the next king.'"

"So what happened?" asked Sonja.

The Value of the Empire

"That night the king was killed, and the next king received the spoils.

"Is this story historical," asked Diana, "or poetic?"

"Good question. I'd say the prose is a mixture of history and symbolism. So what did you all get out of it.?"

"Stay away from liquor," laughed Scott.

"Be careful what we worship," said Dan. "Of all the things about nature we work to conserve, we should probably be concerned not to idolize them."

Sonja said, "I liked the scales of justice. Without referring to scripture, I'll try to bring that story alive by talking about climate action as something we are failing to do. I might even phrase it as 'Can you see the writing on the wall?'"

"I think we're ready for the final story, as the prelude comes to an end, and the apocalyptic visions begin. The new king was preparing to appoint Daniel over the whole kingdom, but that made others jealous. Finding no grounds for complaint, because Daniel was faithful, they decided to look at the laws of his God. In very short order, they found something. They went to the king and said, 'We believe you should establish an ordinance, that whoever prays to anyone other than you, should be thrown into a den of Eurasian brown bears.' So the king signed the document and set the ordinance into action.

"Now Daniel wasn't afraid of anyone, so he continued to pray, and rather defiantly, he prayed in front of his open window. Sure enough, the conspirators came and found him breaking the ordinance. They ran as fast as they could to the king and reported this heinous activity. The king was saddened by this turn of events, but he felt he had no choice. So he ordered that Daniel should be thrown into the bear's den."

"These are feeling more like stories," said Diana.

The Value of the Empire

"At the king's command, Daniel was thrown in, but at least he thoughtfully said, 'May your God, whom you faithfully serve, deliver you!" A stone was placed in front of the cave, and the king had it sealed with his signet ring. Then the king went to his palace and spent the night fasting. At daybreak, the king hurried to the lion's den and called out, 'Daniel, has your God been able to rescue you?' The king nearly fell down in shock when Daniel said 'yes,' and then he gave orders to have Daniel removed.

"So Daniel was removed and found to be unscathed. The king then ordered those who had accused Daniel were to be thrown into the bear's den, and no, it didn't go well for them. Then the king made a decree that:

> 'In all in my royal dominion people should tremble
> and fear before the God of Daniel:
> For he is the living God, enduring forever.
> His kingdom shall never be destroyed,
> and his dominion has no end.
> He delivers and rescues, he works signs and
> wonders in heaven and on earth;
> for he has saved Daniel from the bears.'

"Is that the end of the story?" asked Sonja. I said yes, so she commented that, "I really liked the civil disobedience."

"Please say more," I requested.

"You know, when Daniel was not only afraid of nobody, but he also acted with defiance."

"We have to be careful with that attitude," said Dan. "Doing the right thing has to take into consideration funding."

"Agree to disagree," said Sonja, in a properly defiant way.

"I thought the king was pathetic," said Diana. "He caved in

to the conspirators because he felt he was trapped between a rock and a hard place. I can't begin to tell you how many times I felt that way, when trying to protect the Apache Highlands, and meeting resistance from people who thought it was their land. I've learned to forge ahead doing the right thing. Come to think of it, I guess I was acting like Daniel."

"Great! I think we're now ready to experience some apocalyptic visions. The big difference between the stories and the visions is that the stories were about the king's dreams and the visions are about Daniel's dreams. Here's how the first vison starts: 'Daniel had a dream dancing in his head.'"

"Was it sugar plums?" asked Jameson.

The group groaned, and I said with a smile, "Always a thoughtful contribution from my son. What Daniel says is that there were four winds stirring up the sea, and four beasts rising to the surface. The first looked like a lion with eagles' wings, but the wings were plucked off. It was made to stand on the ground with two feet like a human, and a human mind was given to it."

"Let me try an interpretation," said Rebecca, "because it sounds like a storm trying to control a beast. I only say that because that's how I feel sometimes when I'm trying to protect Phoenix from the ravages of heat."

"Same here," said Dan, "about our conservation efforts."

"Okay," I said. "A second beast looked like a bear with three tusks in its mouth. It was told to 'devour many bodies.'"

Sonja said, "Sounds like what our climate is doing to us."

"Next, a leopard appeared, with wings and four heads, and it was given dominion."

"Reminds me," said Scott, "of our battles for the forests, because we need to be caretakers, not dominators. In other words, fight the beast!"

The Value of the Empire

I might have frowned a little before saying, "The fourth beast was exceedingly strong..."

"You'd lose that battle, Scott," teased Diana.

"The fourth beast had ten horns with eyes like human eyes, and a mouth speaking arrogantly." Scott started to say something, but Dan stopped him, and I continued. "What Daniel saw were thrones being set in place, and an Ancient of Days took his seat on a throne. His clothing was white as snow, and his throne had fiery flames. A court served him, and a book was opened. As Daniel watched, the beast was put to death. As for the other beasts, their dominion was taken away. Then Daniel saw one like a human being coming with the clouds of heaven. And he came to the Ancient of Days and was presented before him. To him was given dominion and glory and kingship, that all should serve him."

"That would be Dan," claimed Diana.

"No," said Dan. "That would be The Nature Conservancy."

An applause rang out, then I said, "Daniel wanted to know the truth of his vision about the fourth, terrifying beast. This is what was said, 'A fourth kingdom shall be different from the others. It shall devour the earth, and speak words against the Most High, and attempt to change the law. They shall be given into his power for a time, then the court shall sit in judgment, and his dominion taken away. The kingship shall be given to the people of the Most High; their kingdom shall be an everlasting kingdom, and all dominions shall serve and obey them."

"That's just the first vision?" asked Rebecca.

"Yes, so what do you think of it?"

"Well, of course there are biblical things to get from it, but I see a vision of hope for the disenfranchised. That's what we fight for in our Building Healthy Cities program."

The Value of the Empire

Sonja said, "Peace and justice may seem like religious programs, but my Climate Action is all about fighting for the good of the world."

"If that vision was considered a doomsday apocalypse," said Scott, "then I'd see it being fulfilled in the out of control forest fires we now have. Maybe we can use this vision as a story of hope, that end times have not yet come, and it's our responsibility to see that they never do."

"Well spoken," said Dan.

"Looks like we're ready for the second vision, and it's as strange as they come. Daniel saw himself in Toledo, the capital of Spain."

"I thought," said Scott, "that Madrid was the capital of Spain."

"Toledo was, until 1561, when King Philip II moved the court to Madrid. Our story takes place during the Aztec exile in Spain, which started in 1521. Daniel specifically saw himself by Rio Manzanares, when he looked up and saw a ram. It had two horns, but one was smaller than the other, and the ram charged all around. Then a male goat appeared from the west, flying just above the ground. The goat had a horn between its eyes, and it ran at the ram with a savage force, and the ram was trampled under foot. Then the goat grew, but at its height of power, its horn was broken. In its place grew four more horns. One grew great, cast truth to the ground, and overthrew the sanctuary. Then a holy one asked, 'How long will this last?' Another holy one said, 'For a long time, but the sanctuary will finally be restored.'

Rebecca said, "I guess that vision is one of hope."

"Then listen to this. Daniel got help from the angel Gabriel, to understand the vision. He said, 'The vision is for the time of the end. As for the ram with two horns, these are the kings of Media and Persia. The goat is the king of Greece, and the four horns that grew are the four kingdoms. At the end of their rule, a king of bold countenance shall arise. He shall grow strong in power, cause fearful destruction, and succeed in what he does. He shall destroy the powerful, and make deceit prosper, and in his own mind he shall be great. But he shall be broken, and not by human hands.'"

"That's creepy," said Diana.

Rebecca said, "I homed in on the idea of the goat casting truth to the ground. My mind missed the rest of what you said, but I'll definitely use this idea of truth. Our task is to lift it up, and speak against those who cast it to the ground."

"I liked the idea," said Scott, "that the sanctuary will finally be restored. I know that forest fires in and of themselves are a useful part of Mother Nature, but we complicate things with our willful disregard for the environment."

Dan said, "What I like is that this vision doesn't give in to fatalism. What we at The Nature Conservancy believe is that mistakes have consequences, and our efforts are to minimize mistakes."

"The imagery was interesting," Sonja said. "Rams and goats fight by locking their horns, and sometimes I feel like I'm locking horns with the climate hoaxers. So I guess what I'm trying to say is that I agree with Dan. It is easy to give in to fatalism, so what I'm taking away from this is a renewed appreciation of the difficulty it is to change minds."

"Wonderful, and that brings us to revolution. The third vision is about Daniel's interpretation of the prophet Jeremiah, where he believes the total devastation of Tenochtitlan will take seventy years. This caused Daniel to seek further understanding through prayer. 'We have sinned and done wrong, acted wickedly and rebelled, turning aside from your commandments. We have not listened to your prophets, and the shame is our own. We have not obeyed the voice of the LORD our God by following his laws, which he set before us by his servants the prophets.'"

"I'll never use the word 'sin,'" said Scott, "but I might try to tell a story about the wrongdoing of not listening to our concerns."

"Good," I said, then continued Daniel's speech: "All of Mexico has sinned, so the curse has been poured on us. A terrible calamity has come, and we have not sought the favor of the LORD our God. You, O LORD, are right in all you do. We are the ones who are wrong, for we have disobeyed your voice."

"Hum," said Scott. "When fires are started by people, whether by accident or on purpose, maybe we need to capitalize on the actual wrongdoing. That way we can focus on the fact that it was wrong, and what we are trying to do is what is right."

"Good. Storytelling as a sermon is supposed to end with good news, but storytelling about nature can have any end you want. Now, where was I?" I paused for a bit, and Sonja said that it had something to do with disobedience. "Thanks. Here's how it continued: 'O Lord, in view of all the good acts you have done in the past for us, your people, I pray that you would turn your wrath away from your holy city Tenochtitlan. O Lord, let your face shine upon your desolated sanctuary. I do not make this request on the ground of our righteousness, but on the ground of your mercy.'"

"Interesting," said Dan, "but what's the difference between righteousness and mercy?"

The Value of the Empire

"Jameson," I said, "could you Google that for us?"

He quickly pulled out his phone and announced "righteousness is about being morally correct and justifiable, while mercy is about benevolence, forgiveness, and kindness."

Dan said, "Righteousness sounds more secular to me and mercy sounds more sacred. I think I could talk about the morality of failing to care for nature."

After a short pause, I said, "While Daniel was praying, the angel Gabriel once again showed up. He said, 'Daniel, I have now come out to give you wisdom and understanding. Seventy weeks are decreed for your people, to put an end to sin, and to atone for iniquity, to bring in everlasting righteousness. So know this: from the time that the word went out to restore and rebuild Tenochtitlan until the time of an anointed one, there shall be seventy weeks. And for sixty-two weeks it shall be built again with streets and moat, but it will be a troubled time.' Okay, your thoughts?"

"I never thought of myself as a prophet," said Sonja, "but I'm beginning to see my job as prophetic."

"What I got out of the confessional prayer," said Rebecca, "was that change takes more than confession. It needs to be followed by action. I'm so caught up in action, that maybe I need to prepare my own work with confessions of my own mistakes."

Dan said, "I think what I'll remember most about this vision is that one can hold out hope in the darkest of times. I don't want to get there, but I fear we are headed that way. My expectation of the future is to cast a positive vision, which I believe we have through The Nature Conservancy. I know it's not all good right now, but somebody once said, Sunday's coming."

"That's about Jim Caldwell," blurted out Jameson.

Some smiles made their way around the room, but I think

it was mostly because I didn't try to make this storytelling an evangelistic moment. "That brings us to the final vision. It was revealed as a true word about a great conflict. Daniel was standing on the bank of a river when he looked up and saw a man clothed in linen. His face was like lightning, his eyes like flaming torches, his arms and legs like bronze, and his voice was like a roaring multitude. When he heard this voice he fell into a trance, but a hand touched him and brought him to his hands and knees."

"I thought maybe it would bring him to his senses," laughed Scott.

"He said, 'Daniel, pay attention to my words, and stand on your feet. Do not fear, Daniel, for from the first day that you set your mind to gain understanding and to humble yourself before your God, your words have been heard. I have now come to help you understand what is to happen to your people at the end of days. Do not fear, greatly beloved, you are safe. Be strong and courageous! Do you know why I have come to you? I am to tell you what is inscribed in the book of truth. Three more kings shall arise, but the fourth will be richer than all of them. Then a warrior king shall arise, who shall rule with great domination and take action as he pleases. And while still rising in power, his kingdom shall be broken. Then the king of the south shall grow strong, but one of his officers shall grow stronger than he and shall rule a realm greater than his own. After some years they shall make an alliance. In those times a branch shall rise up who will take action against them and prevail. Even their gods shall be carried off as spoils of war. His sons shall wage war and assemble a multitude of great forces. The king of the south shall go out and do battle against the king of the north, but he will be defeated. Then the king of the north

The Value of the Empire

shall rise against the king of the south.'"

Now I must admit that this vision was so long, I was reading it, so I stopped for a moment and looked around. I saw confusion, frustration, and some intrigue, so I continued in a more storytelling way. "In those times many will fight the king of the south, but he will not prevail. The king will come with strength, and he will bring terms of peace." I paused again, then said, "Next, a whole bunch of war stories happen, but I won't bother you with them. Picking the vision back up, the king did as he pleased. He exalted himself and considered himself greater than any god, and spoke horrendous things against the God of gods. He shall do well until the period of wrath is completed, for what is determined will be done. At the end, the king of the south will attack and lose. Then the king of the south will settle on the holy mountain, and he will come to his end, with no one to help him.

"Ready for the last bit of the vision?" They nodded yes, so I said, 'After great anguish, your people will be delivered. Those who are wise shall shine like the brightness of the sky, and those who lead many to righteousness, like the stars forever and ever. However, many will be running back and forth, and evil will increase.' Then he said to Daniel, 'Go your way, for the words are to remain secret and sealed until the time of the end. Many will be purified, cleansed, and refined, but the wicked will continue to act wickedly. Those who are wise will understand. Happy are those who persevere, but go your way and rest. You will rise for your reward at the end of the days.' Okay. We made it. I'm ready for comments."

There was a bit of a lull, as people were processing what they could, then Dan spoke up. "Obviously, The Nature Conservancy can't use the religious connotations, but I liked a

The Value of the Empire

lot of the vision. The ending was very useful. It is good for us to remember that the wicked won't change, so it is our job to be wise, but what did the vision say the wise would do?"

Looking back at my Bible, I said, "Understand."

"Yep," said Scott. "That's our job. If we don't understand what's going on in nature, how could we expect others to understand?"

Dan then continued, "I also liked the bit about persevering, because it is the road to happiness. And the bit about going your own way and resting, I think that's an important secret for all of us here. We need to find that natural balance of work and rest."

"Thanks," I said. "Any other thoughts about the rest of the final vision?"

"It was too much, suggested Sonja. "Maybe you could lift out what you see as important, then we can offer our thoughts about those."

"Okay. What did you think about Daniel being told: 'Do not fear. You are safe. Be strong and courageous!'"

Diana said, "I don't want people to feel safe. I want them to be afraid about not conserving our land and water."

Rebecca said, "What I get out of it is that we need to be strong and courageous."

"So," I asked, "what do you think about a book of truth?"

Dan said, "It's very interesting how the past few years have seen a lot of questioning truth. To me, a book of truth is a book of science, but it seems that facts are falling out of favor."

"I agree," said Sonja. "Trying to educate people about our work on climate action has been challenging. I think it's because people these days work more out of their feelings than their thoughts."

"The vision talks about an alliance forming, but a branch

The Value of the Empire

would rise up, take action and prevail. Thoughts about that?"

Scott said, "It does seem like evil alliances get formed against our work, so I like the idea of us being the branch that takes action and prevails."

"Okay. What about this one? Those who are wise shall shine like the brightness of the sky."

Dan said, "I'm motivated to get us to have more media coverage. Maybe that wisdom would help our cause to shine bright."

"Great. I think that is a good note to end our time on. I can't thank you enough for giving up your morning for this unique experience in storytelling. I hope your stories will be told in better and better ways, so they can be heard and understood."

A kind round of applause ended the morning, and Dan gave an extra comment of appreciation. Each of the others shook my hand and said thanks, while the general tenor of their thoughts was that of surprise that it sort of worked. Jameson and I then got in the car for our thirty minute ride home. "So what did you think of all that, Jameson?"

"The whole thing was a bit of a blur for me. I preferred the stories of Ezra, Nehemiah and Chronicles, but Daniel leaves something to the imagination," he said with a grin. "I guess my question for you, Dad, is whether or not you believe in angels, since Daniel's stories had quite a few."

"As a Caldwellian, I believe in the spirit world, and maybe even more so, I believe that I don't know everything there is to know about the spirit world."

"I hear students at school talking about angelology," said Jameson. "They understand there's no developed doctrine, but many have experienced seeing angels."

"Certainly better than experiences seeing demons," I said.

The Value of the Empire

"Another question I have," said Jameson, "from hearing Daniel, is about warfare."

"Well, this is a different kind of warfare," I explained. "It's called spiritual warfare, which is a battle against evil spirits."

"Like alcohol?"

"It certainly can be, but this kind of evil spirit is from the spiritual realm."

"Okay, one last question. I remember in my high school economics class when the teacher said, 'Never forget this. Everything boils down to money.' Do you agree, Dad?"

"It's a rather disheartening thought, but right in too many ways. What I don't like about it is that truth isn't about money."

"What is truth about?"

"Remember when Dan suggested the difference between mercy and righteousness was that one is secular and the other sacred?"

"No."

"Well, first of all, nice job of listening." I said with a grin.

"So, what's your point?" Jameson asked with intrigue.

"You asked if I believe everything boils down to money, and my answer is no. Perhaps the secular answer is yes, but the sacred answer is that truth isn't about money."

"So what is truth about?"

"Truth is something we all need to find on our own. As a Caldwellian, I find truth in the resurrection. That truth rises above, if you will, any earthly powers. It gives the kind of hope that can never be defeated, because even death doesn't defeat the believer." About that time we rolled into the driveway, and were warmly welcomed by Sol.

I told her that I wanted her to come with us on our final trip to Flagstaff. She smiled and said, "Okay," and Jameson and I

The Value of the Empire

were ecstatic. Now I had a month to think about the last five books for our Old Testament experiences. I had heard they are known as the Megillot, and now I was getting excited to hear about them from an Aztec in an Aztec synagogue. That night I drifted off to sleep with a flurry of memories from our first two trips to Mexico, and the new understandings I had gained thus far from these experiential education excursions.

ACT IV
Liturgies in Flagstaff

The Value of the Empire

SCENE ONE
Lamentations, Ecclesiastes

We had a 9 a.m. appointment with Atzi, a docent at the beautiful Flagstaff Aztec Synagogue, but I was losing hope that we would make it on time. My plan was to rise and shine at 6 a.m., and hit the road by 7 at the latest, to make the two hour journey. It was now 6:50, Jameson and I were ready to go, and Sol was nowhere to be found. After repeatedly calling, she emerged from the bedroom closet with two dresses in tow. "Which one do you think I should wear?" she asked innocently. Pointing to the one on the left, I said, "We're getting in the car. Please hurry."

Sol responded, "Mi amor. You seem to forget that I work on MST (Mexican Standard Time)."

Don't get me wrong, I love my wife. Sol is truly my soul mate, and the best thing that ever happened to me. But when it comes to timeliness, she stresses me, because I don't ever like to be late. That's just one way we grew up differently. As we got in the car, Jameson kindly suggested that I needed to chill. It was a good reminder, and Sol actually got in the car a little before 7.

The trip up I-17 to Flagstaff is the kind where you hold your breath. In just over one hundred miles, you ascend a series of mountains, going from one thousand feet above sea level in Phoenix to over seven thousand feet in Flagstaff. That's more than a mile of climbing, and the car acts like it. My hybrid chugs up the mountain about as well as I do on foot, but the experiences are far more than that. The road is narrow and has lots of turns, and the drivers act like they're in a road race.

The Value of the Empire

The other way you inhale is with the breath-taking views. The wonderful Sonoran saguaros are an icon of the American Southwest, and they are plentifully in view as the journey northward begins. After about three thousand feet of elevation, the saguaros give way to scrub brush, but the lengthy views across the landscape are beautiful. Jagged mountains on the other side of expansive valleys are postcard picturesque. At about five thousand feet, the beginnings of pine country come into sight. Even though I hate I-17, the geographic changes along the way make the trip enjoyable.

When it was all said and done, we pulled up to the Synagogoue at 8:58 and went in. The receptionist greeted us, and after identifying myself, she said that Atzi was waiting for us. She escorted us back to Atzi's office, where a pleasant woman in her late fifties stood up and greeted us. "Good morning, my name is Atzi. I'm looking forward to chatting this morning with you about the Megillot." We then introduced ourselves, and Jameson asked about her name. She responded, "It is an Aztec word that means rain, and it's reserved for those who can't help but splash in the puddles." A surprisingly impish smile spread across her face before saying, "Enough about me. Let's move down the hallway to the first of the five scrolls we have on display. They are copies, but the originals were lost in the destruction of Tenochtitlan."

She stopped before getting to the first exhibition window, and turned around in good docent style to speak. "Megillot is the Aztec word for five scrolls, imitating the five books of the Law, as do the five books of the Psalms. What I find interesting is that several of the books had trouble getting into the final canon of the Aztec Scriptures." That same impish grin all of a sudden spread from cheek bone to cheek bone. When Sol

The Value of the Empire

asked what her smile was about, Atzi said, "I just relate to the trouble makers in the Megillot, because I wanted to become an Aztec priest, and as you know, women aren't allowed. I guess that's why I decided to become a docent. I love my faith, my religion, and my Synagogue, and hang on to hope that I might someday be fully included." Sol stepped forward and hugged her in a way that only a person who has lived with exclusion their whole life could understand.

Atzi was obviously moved by this kindness, then asked Sol about her religious upbringing. "My parents are from Mexico, and I was raised in the Aztec faith. While I was still young, my parents moved to America, and my mother was converted to the Caldwellian faith. It is really the only faith I remember, but the prejudice I have experienced as a Mexican-American woman is unforgettable."

All four of us stood there in silence for a moment, then Atzi continued her docent-trained talk. "The five writings we'll be looking at this morning gained importance after the return from exile in Spain by being read during holidays. The Song of Solomon is used at the Passover Feast. Ruth is read for Pentecost, the Aztec holiday celebrating the giving of the Law to Abund on Mount Cerro Raxon. Lamentations is solemnly read on the 9th of Av, which is the date Templo Mayor was destroyed in Tenochtitlan. Ecclesiastes is liturgically employed at the Feast of Tabernacles, a time when we remember our ancestors wandering in the wilderness for a long time, and Esther is used at the Feast of Purim, commemorating the defeat of Haman's plot to massacre the Aztecs."

Atzi then turned and we followed her to the first display window, which was surprisingly large. The glass-enclosed environment was backlit with a medium bright light, which Atzi explained was to protect the book.

"I have a question," stated Jameson. "I thought the five scrolls would be, you know, scrolls."

"Not a question," smiled Atzi, "but I'll answer anyway. The originals were scrolls, but since the invention of the printing press, copies started being made into books. This is the first book we'll talk about," she then turned to the side so we could all move up to the glass, "and it's called Lamentations.

Lamentations

"This book is a collection of five poetic laments written after the fall of Tenochtitlan, to express the grief and despair of the people. For me, the beauty of the book is that it gives permission to vent anger, even at God. In other words, there is nothing that we cannot bring to divine attention."

"That's amazing," said Sol. "I never believed it was okay to get mad at God."

"Where did you go wrong with that Caldwellian faith?" Atzi asked with a mild grin. It was about that time I realized I would have to pay attention, because these two were really connecting. I think Atzi was being genuinely interested in learning when she asked, "So Jim Caldwell gives you permission to get angry with the LORD?"

"Well, I'd say its permission from Pablo. When he was writing about the New Life in Jim, he said, 'Be angry but do not sin' (Ephesians 4:26). For me that suggests that God has big shoulders and can take our pain. It's certainly better to get anger out than to keep it in."

"But isn't that sin?"

The Value of the Empire

"Not at all," replied Sol. "Keeping it in can destroy a person, and I would call that a sin. Anyway, I heard a sermon once that said, 'All sin is wrongdoing, but not all wrongdoing is sin.'"

"Okay," said Jameson. "I'm lost."

Sol said, "Wrongdoing is the big picture, while sin is just a part of it."

"Still confused," I said.

Sol explained, "You can exceed the speed limit while driving here, and that is against the law. It's wrongdoing, but it's not a sin." She then looked at Atzi and said, "You are being excluded from the priesthood. I would call that a sin rather than wrongdoing."

We all just stood there stunned for a moment, then Atzi said, "So I can be angry about my exclusion, but I should be careful not to sin?"

"Yes!" said Sol. "That's what you just said is the beauty of the book of Lamentations. We can feel free to even be angry at God, because it's not a wrong thing to do. In my opinion, the sin would come in if you don't push to make things right in the Aztec faith."

"Nice segue," said Atzi. "I guess its time to get back to the book. Lamentations gives voice to the reason for the disaster known as the Exile, and offers the balance of promise. Dwelling on Cortés conquering the Aztecs, it's called a theology of doom. It is when the returned deportees expressed grief, despair, and alienation from God, prior to the rebuilding of Templo Mayor and the city of Tenochtitlan. It is about blaming God and asking questions like 'Why me?' It is mostly about feelings, so the way out is to start thinking. This balances us through a theology of hope, which entails confession, submission, and loyalty.

"Here's a quick overview. Chapter 1 is a dirge over the dead

The Value of the Empire

city Tenochtitlan. It is impossible to fathom the pain they felt upon returning from Spain and seeing the disaster that used to be the holiest place in the world. Chapter 2 is a cry to God for mercy, because the poet believes the LORD used justifiable anger in the assault of Tenochtitlan. Chapter 3 is a personal lament and prayer, expressing confidence in God's steadfast love and faithfulness. Chapter 4 is a recounting of the suffering and hardships endured by the survivors, and Chapter 5 is a community psalm of lament and a prayer for mercy during restoration."

Sol asked, "So how is this dirge meaningful to you?"

"Because," Atzi replied, "it is a search for meaning in suffering."

"And has it helped you?"

"It has caused me to think that even God lamented the fall and destruction of Tenochtitlan."

"How did you come to that conclusion?" asked Sol.

"For me, it comes in Lamentations 3:19-24, which says:

> The thought of my affliction and my
> homelessness is wormwood and gall!
> My soul continually thinks of it
> and is bowed down within me.
> But this I call to mind,
> and therefore I have hope:
> The steadfast love of the LORD never ceases,
> his mercies never come to an end;
> they are new every morning;
> great is your faithfulness.
> 'The LORD is my portion,' says my soul,
> 'therefore I will hope in him.'"

The Value of the Empire

"Amen!" proclaimed a smiling Sol.

"Love it!" offered Jameson. "But what did you say was the liturgical purpose of Lamentations?"

Atzi smiled with patience and said, "It is used at the annual Aztec commemoration of the ninth of Av, the date when the city finally fell to Cortés. So yes, it is a very sad reading, intended to be cathartic. Just listen to how it begins." She then opened a Bible she was carrying and read it aloud: "'How lonely sits the city that once was full of people! How like a widow she has become, she that was great among the nations! She that was a princess among the provinces has become a vassal.' (Lamentations 1:1). What is sad to me, is that the city's downfall is considered to be its sinfulness."

"Why is that sad?" asked Sol.

"Because, deserved or not, the author's blame of Tenochtitlan seems hardly useful for moving on. I give in to the thought only because confession of sin is necessary before healing can begin. My frustration is that I get tired of pretending I have never confessed."

"Oh, I get it," said Sol. "My church sometimes has congregational confessions that I don't feel any particular need to confess."

"Thanks," said Atzi, "That also feels real, and the poem certainly gets real. Listen to these verses from the second chapter: 'Look, O LORD, and consider! To whom have you done this? Should women eat their offspring, the children they have borne? Should priest and prophet be killed in the sanctuary of the Lord? The young and the old are lying on the ground in the streets; my young women and my young men have fallen by the sword; in the day of your anger you have killed them, slaughtering without mercy. You invited my enemies from all around as if for a day of festival; and on the day of the anger of the LORD no one escaped or survived; those whom I bore and reared my enemy has destroyed.' (Lamentations 2:20-22)."

"That's terrible!" complained Jameson.

"What I really like," continued Atzi without acknowledgment of what Jameson had just said, "is the hope part from chapter three that I already mentioned. Here's how it continues: 'The LORD is good to those who wait for him, to the soul that seeks him. It is good that one should wait quietly for the salvation of the LORD.' (3:25-26)." Atzi then looked at Sol and said, "That's me, when it comes to my relationship with this Synagogue. I wait quietly for God's salvation to make things equal and right. I wouldn't say this to most people here, but I especially relate to 3:49-51. 'My eyes will flow without ceasing, without respite, until the LORD from heaven looks down and sees. My eyes cause me grief at the fate of all the young women in my city.'"

"Wow," said Sol, as she slowly bowed her head. "I think I'll start praying for you, and all of us who suffer."

Atzi graciously acknowledged this kindness, then said, "Now imagine the dereliction of duty pronounced in chapter four. Verse 1 talks about the sacred stones lying scattered in the streets. Don't forget that this was their Promised Land. They never believed God would let them lose it, so they blamed God. You know it's much easier to blame than to be responsible. Verse 4 describes the 'tongue of the infant sticks to the roof of its mouth for thirst; the children beg for food, but no one gives them anything.'"

I mentioned that it reminded me of the children in Ukraine and Gaza, but Atzi wanted to continue. "'Those who feasted on delicacies perish in the streets; those who were brought up in purple cling to ash heaps' (vs. 5). 'Now their visage is blacker than soot; they are not recognized in the streets. Their skin has shriveled on their bones; it has become as dry as wood.' (vs. 8). Then the blame returns: 'The LORD gave full vent to his wrath; he poured out his hot anger, and kindled a fire that consumed the foundations of Tenochtitlan' (vs. 11)." The visceral reaction I was getting was making me want to ask Atzi to stop, when I realized that was the purpose of the reading. If it's memorable, we are less likely to forget.

Atzi droned on, at least in my mind. Obviously she was giving us a liturgical experience that required extreme solemnity, but for some reason I just wasn't in the mood. Then she said, "'The LORD himself has scattered them, he will regard them no more; no honor was shown to the priests, no favor to the elders'" (vs. 16). Jameson started to say something, but Sol and I both gave him the stare. "Here's how this chapter ends. 'The punishment of your iniquity is accomplished, he will keep you in exile no longer; but your iniquity he will punish, he will uncover your sins' (vs. 22).

"There is one final chapter, and it serves as a closing communal lament. 'Remember, O LORD, what has befallen us; look, and see our disgrace! Our inheritance has been turned over to strangers, our home to aliens' (5:1-2). Here's one that's quite poignant: 'Our ancestors sinned; they are no more, and we bear their iniquities' (5:7). And another: 'The joy of our hearts has ceased; our dancing has been turned to mourning. The crown has fallen from our head; woe to us, for we have sinned! Because of this our hearts are sick, because of these things our eyes have grown dim' (5:15-17).

"Are we done yet?" asked a weary Jameson.

"No. "Here's how it closes: 'Why have you forgotten us

The Value of the Empire

completely? Why have you forsaken us these many days? Restore us to yourself, O LORD, that we may be restored; renew our days as of old—unless you have utterly rejected us, and are angry with us beyond measure' (5:20-22). Any thoughts?"

Jameson said, "Well, if I can speak now, it felt like a roller coaster of emotions."

"I'm drained," said Sol.

My thoughts wanted to take a back seat, but I went ahead and said, "The hope is easier to take than the despair. I suppose it's good to have an annual time of remembrance. The community can gather and experience what they need, because it seems to all be there. Anyway, thank you very much, Atzi. Can we take a quick restroom break before moving to the next window?"

Ecclesiastes

When we regathered, Atzi took us to the next window. "Can you get the book out for us to look at it closer?" asked Jameson.

Atzi said, "I was hoping there would be that level of interest. Few visitors ever make that request, but these are copies, so the answer is yes." She then retrieved a key from her pocket and gingerly opened the window. "Keep in mind that this is still a part of our Sacred Scriptures, so we must show reverence and appreciation." She then pulled the book from its stand and said, "Follow me."

Sol said, "Sounds intriguingly like Jim Caldwell."

We went to a small room and Atzi turned on the lights. We all sat down at a table and Atzi lovingly opened the book of

The Value of the Empire

Ecclesiastes. Jameson said, "Say more about the scroll stuff."

"This is a copy. The originals are gone, just like I said." I was getting a little frustrated, because I sensed prejudice against Jameson and myself. Finding equality wasn't the purpose of our visit, so I let it go, and Atzi went on. "Over the nearly five hundred years since the stories were told, they slowly made their way into book form." Atzi then read the first verse, "'The words of the Teacher, the son of Montezuma, king in Tenochtitlan.' This is probably a false claim, because the words used are from a much later time. The Aztec word for teacher is *Qoheleth*. The person was probably an important official in Tenochtitlan who expressed views of an elite group of people. He or she (*Qoheleth* is the feminine form of the word) counseled acceptance of the current economic and social conditions, because opposition was useless.

"Let me go back for a moment. There's just so much to say about this book, that I get a bit excited when talking about it. Here's some of the things I love about the book. I view *Qoheleth* as a practical theologian, because he or she is honest about the ways of God in the world, then instructs the listeners on how to live. In a strange way, the book helps to discern God's will. If you are a pessimist, you'll find God talking to you in this book. Likewise, if you're an optimist, you'll find God's Spirit nurturing you. In my opinion, that's the power of the book. It honestly addresses the tensions inherent in life, by embracing them, and then confessing that life is still better than death.

"Here's the structure of the book. The first two chapters decry experience, while the third chapter admits that humans cannot know the times. Chapter 4 is about human relationships and the fifth chapter suggests that wise people revere God. Chapters six and seven recommend enjoying what is good because it is fleeting, while chapter 8 complains that the meaning of life is hidden. The ninth chapter says that fate is random, while chapter 10 offers observations on life. The eleventh chapter says to enjoy life, or at least youthfulness, and it ends with a talk about the end of life.

"Okay, one more thing. This book is read each year during the Feast of Tabernacles, a seven-day holiday that appears in the book of Leviticus. Since the book relates to issues of doubt, it is a proper reading for that feast. It is a time when we remember the struggles our ancestors had wandering in the wilderness, and their groanings and lack of faith. Here at the Flagstaff Aztec Synagogue, the more daring of us build shelters in the parking lot and camp out."

"Do you do that, Atzi?" asked Jameson.

"Yes, I do, from about 10 a.m. to 7 p.m. We cook lunch on open fires, play games during the day, then cook and eat dinner. Most of us go to our nice comfortable homes for the evening, but the youth group usually camps out all night."

"Why do you still celebrate it?" asked Sol.

"It is obviously a very important festival because it is mentioned often in our Aztec Scriptures. It was during the Feast that Templo Mayor was dedicated, and again at the rededication of the Temple under the leadership of Joshua and Zerubbabel. Ezra read the Word of God during the Feast in the book of Nehemiah. And I dare say that it was during the Feast that your own Jim Caldwell said, 'If anyone thirsts, let him come to me and drink' (John 7:37)."

Jameson smiled and said, "That's pretty cool."

"Let's get back to the book. After the introductory verse, the author's theme is revealed: 'Vanity of vanities, says the Teacher, vanity of vanities! All is vanity' (1:2). *Qoheleth* uses

The Value of the Empire

the word vanity because the original Aztec word is vapor, which is figurative for worthless. Can't you just see this person debating in a public assembly? I sense anger from the words, where he is almost taunting people to disagree with him. Like, 'Go ahead and say anything you want, because you have no chance to win this argument.'"

"Can't that word also be translated as breath?" I asked.

"Yes," said Atzi, with a surprised look on her face. "In that sense, it's like the teacher would be saying 'I won't waste my breath.'"

Jameson said, "That's grim."

Atzi agreed. "It's a painful way to express the thought that we never know if we will be alive from one moment to the next."

Sol said, "Please tell me it doesn't mean that life isn't worth living."

"I don't think so. As negative as the book begins, it does celebrate some good things, but not right away. Verse three asks, 'What do people gain from all the toil at which they toil under the sun?'"

"Why were they so negative?" asked Jameson.

"Don't forget that the book was compiled after my people returned from exile. They had unbelievable work ahead of them, and it must have made them angry that they had been taken into exile in the first place. The feelings continue to be expressed in verse eight: 'All things are wearisome; more than one can express.'"

Jameson said, "I can just see people listening to *Qoheleth*, and thinking that there was nothing to debate about. When you're right, you're right."

"Maybe," said Atzi, "just maybe, and that might be why the Teacher hammered away with verse 14: 'I saw all the deeds that are done under the sun; and see, all is vanity and a chasing after wind.'"

"I prefer that metaphor," said Sol. "When I was growing up, we dried our clothes outside on a clothesline. When the wind would kick up and blow some of the clothes off the line, there was nothing we could do except pick them up. We could chase after the clothes, but chasing after wind is nonsense."

Atzi said, "Here's another level of understanding about the wind metaphor. It's that we can't discern God's spirit or purpose in our lives."

"I disagree," said Jameson. "I'm thinking about going into the ministry because I feel God's spirit calling me."

"There you have it!" proclaimed a rather excited Atzi.

"Huh?" asked Jameson.

"A debate!"

We smiled and laughed a bit before Atzi said, "But remember that Ecclesiastes spends its first half with negativity." She then carefully turned the page and asked Jameson to read 2:11. "But before you do, the context of the verse is a bit of bragging about the Teacher's accomplishments. Okay, let's hear the words."

Jameson readied himself for the assignment and said, "'Then I considered all that my hands had done and the toil I had spent in doing it, and again, all was vanity and a chasing after wind, and there was nothing to be gained under the sun.' Reminds me of the old saying, 'There's no need for a U-Haul at a gravesite.'"

After a mild frown, Sol asked, "May I read something?"

"Of course. Why don't you move to where the book is, rather than moving the book to where you are?" Sol exchanged places with Jameson and Atzi said, "Please read 2:24-26."

The Value of the Empire

Sol rubbed her eyes, then read, "'There is nothing better for mortals than to eat and drink, and find enjoyment in the r toil. This also, I saw, is from the hand of God; for apart from him who can eat or who can have enjoyment? For to the one who pleases him God gives wisdom and knowledge and joy; but to the sinner he gives the work of gathering and heaping, only to give to one who pleases God. This also is vanity and a chasing after wind.'" She looked up and asked, "Is this a good thing or a bad thing?"

There was a moment of silence until we all four said in almost unity, "Another debate!"

Atzi then looked at me and said, "Your turn." I slid into place as she was saying, "Read 3:1-8."

I looked down and said, "Oh, I like this one."

For everything there is a season,
and a time for every matter under heaven:
a time to be born, and a time to die;
a time to plant, and a time to pluck up what is planted;
a time to kill, and a time to heal;
a time to break down, and a time to build up;
a time to weep, and a time to laugh;
a time to mourn, and a time to dance;
a time to throw away stones, and a time to gather them;
a time to embrace, and a time to refrain from embracing;
a time to seek, and a time to lose;
a time to keep, and a time to throw away;
a time to tear, and a time to sew;
a time to keep silence, and a time to speak;
a time to love, and a time to hate;
a time for war, and a time for peace.

The Value of the Empire

Sol said, "I'm guessing that's not as debatable."

We smiled in agreement and Atzi lovingly pulled the book back towards herself. "Then try this one: 'Better is a poor but wise youth than an old but foolish king, who will no longer take advice. One can indeed come out of prison to reign, even though born poor in the kingdom. I saw all the living who, moving under the sun, follow that youth who replaced the king; there was no end to all those people whom he led. Yet those who come later will not rejoice in him. Surely this also is vanity and a chasing after wind' (4:13-16)."

"Sounds political," I said, "so wouldn't it be nice if we simply used wisdom?"

Sol said, "I'm just glad the Teacher wasn't debating the existence of God. *Qoheleth* was wise enough to just talk about the things people believed about God."

"Very wise, mom. Very wise."

After a moment of appreciative silence, Atzi continued by reading. "There is a grievous ill that I have seen under the sun: riches were kept by their owners to their hurt, and those riches were lost in a bad venture; though they are parents of children, they have nothing in their hands. As they came from their mother's womb, so they shall go again, naked as they came; they shall take nothing for their toil, which they may carry away with their hand. This also is a grievous ill: just as they came, so shall they go; and what gain do they have from toiling for the wind? Besides, all their days they eat in darkness, in much vexation and sickness and resentment" (5:13-17).

Jameson rather excitedly said, "That reminds me of Jim Caldwell's Parable of the Rich Fool."

"Great connection," I said. "Both stories warn about the peril of possessions."

The Value of the Empire

Sol said, "Greed is the biggest problem in America today."

"That brings me to 6:1-2," said Atzi. "There is an evil that I have seen under the sun, and it lies heavy upon humankind: those to whom God gives wealth, possession, and honor, so that they lack nothing of all that they desire, yet God does not enable them to enjoy these things, but a stranger enjoys them. This is vanity; it is a grievous ill."

"I'd be willing to try enjoying wealth," said Jameson with a wink.

Atzi said, "I get it that you're joking, but many people want riches without toil. Here's 6:9, 'Better is the sight of the eyes than the wandering of appetite; this also is vanity and a chasing after wind.'"

My youthful memories in Indiana kicked in and I said, "I kind of liked chasing after tornadoes."

"Yes," said Atzi. "Sometimes wind is good and sometimes it is bad, so the Teacher was suggesting that we should try to know the difference. Maybe that's why *Qoheleth* then moved to proverbial speech. Listen to this one: 'A good name is better than precious ointment, and the day of death, than the day of birth' (7:1). Or even this one: 'Do not be too righteous, and do not act too wise; why should you destroy yourself?' (7:16)."

"Whoa!" said James. "This guy was pretty dark."

"Oh, and it gets darker. Listen to 7:26-28: 'I found more bitter than death the woman who is a trap, whose heart is snares, and nets, whose hands are fetters; one who pleases God escapes her, but the sinner is taken by her. See, this is what I found, says the Teacher, adding one thing to another to find the sum, which my mind has sought repeatedly, but I have not found. One man among a thousand I found, but a woman among all these I have not found.'"

The Value of the Empire

"That seems pretty rude," complained Sol.

"What I found," said Jameson, "was the identity of the Teacher."

"Say more," I requested.

"*Qoheleth* must be a man. Otherwise, why talk so despairingly about a woman?"

"Maybe," said Atzi, "and then again, maybe not. Anyway, try this: 'There is vanity that takes place on earth, that there are righteous people who are treated according to the conduct of the wicked, and there are wicked people who are treated according to the conduct of the righteous. I said that this also is vanity. So I commend enjoyment, for there is nothing better for people under the sun than to eat, and drink, and enjoy themselves, for this will go with them in their toil through the days of life that God gives them under the sun' (8:14-15)."

Jameson smiled and said, "So that's where that comes from. Every once in a while I hear fraternity boys on campus saying to eat, drink, and be merry."

"So you walk right on by, correct?" questioned Sol.

"Mom! Of course, but then again, a little bit of eating and drinking and merriment after a tough class is in order."

"Let's move it along," I implored.

"As does the Teacher. He, or she," said Atzi, with one of those impish grins, "says, 'whoever is joined with all the living has hope, for a living dog is better than a dead lion. The living know that they will die, but the dead know nothing; they have no more reward, and even the memory of them is lost. Their love and their hate and their envy have already perished; never again will they have any share in all that happens under the sun' (9:4-6)."

"It's almost as if," I said, "the author takes death so

seriously, that it somehow gives permission to take life seriously. I would never have guessed that Ecclesiastes was a morality story, but it seems to me that the groundwork is laid to act ethically."

"That may be a stretch," said Atzi, "but certainly worth consideration." I must admit that I once again felt a little put down for being a man, but decided my job here was to listen. "Which brings us to chapter 10." She once again turned the page, capturing our attention. "Here's verses 12-15 'Words spoken by the wise bring them favor, but the lips of fools consume them. The words of their mouth begin in foolishness, and their talk ends in wicked madness; yet fools talk on and on. No one knows what is to happen, and who can tell anyone what the future holds? The toil of fools wears them out, for they do not even know the way to town.'"

Jameson said, "Sounds like a practical ethic to me, Dad."

"Okay," said Atzi. Maybe you'll like this one: 'Just as you do not know how the breath comes to the bones in the mother's womb, so you do not know the work of God, who makes everything' (11:5).

"Yes," said Sol. "We should always defer to God, who is infinitely smarter than us."

"Not to mention, our judge," said Atzi with a surprisingly solemn countenance. "The ninth verse of chapter 11 says, 'Rejoice, young man, while you are young, and let your heart cheer you in the days of your youth. Follow the inclination of your heart and the desire of your eyes, but know that for all these things God will bring you into judgment."

"In other words," said Jameson, "make judgments of your own, but be sure they build up rather than tear down."

Atzi ignored him, then said, "How about 12:5? 'When one

is afraid of heights, and terrors are in the road; the almond tree blossoms, the grasshopper drags itself along and desire fails; because all must go to their eternal home, and the mourners will go about the streets."

"What do you think about that, Atzi?" asked Sol.

"The message I get is to not give in to fear. I like the idea of choosing to notice the blossoming of the almond tree. That doesn't mean to ignore what's going on all around, but to find peace inside. Here's how the book ends: 'Vanity of vanities, says the Teacher; all is vanity' (12:8). An epilogue finishes the book with this intriguing saying, 'Of making many books there is no end, and much study is a weariness of the flesh' (12:8)."

Jameson teasingly said, "I think I have a brand new favorite verse for school." I laughed and Sol frowned, and Atzi suggested taking a break before looking at the final three books.

"Before we take a break, if you don't mind, I have a tradition over the last three summers of occasionally checking in to see what was either learned or appreciated." Atzi nodded that she was fine with that, so I looked at Sol and Jameson and said, "So, what do you think?"

Sol immediately spoke up and said, "I really liked hearing about the holidays the books are associated with. That made them come alive in a wonderful way. I grew up surrounded by the Aztec faith, but I was too young to appreciate the details, and then became a Caldwellian. I also liked that Lamentations gives permission to be angry, even at God, if it's useful."

Jameson said, "I learned a whole new appreciation for Lamentations as a search for meaning in suffering."

I said, "There was something very special to me. Reading Lamentations 3:1-8 from an extraordinary copy of the book, right here in the Flagstaff Aztec Synagogue. I'll never forget it."

The Value of the Empire

Sol said, "I never thought of Ecclesiastes as a debate, and I particularly liked that it's not a debate about God's existence. It's a debate about how people think about God."

"What about you?" I asked as I looked at Atzi.

"I learned that my desire to become an Aztec priest may be little more than striving after wind, so I need to focus on eating, drinking, and being merry, in case it never happens. Anything else?"

"Not from me," said Jameson, "but I do want that restroom break."

SCENE TWO
Solomon, Esther, Ruth

We were all excited to see the other three windows holding the Megillot. Atzi said, "The first two books only took an hour, so we're in great shape to be done by noon. Would you care to have a quick tour of the Synagogue?" We were very interested, so she led us down the hallway to the sanctuary. I was surprised that it wasn't very big, and Atzi noticed my expression. She said, "You know, I'm sure, that we Aztecs are God's people. We were spread all over the world after the exile and some are here, but not very many."

"Why don't you evangelize?" asked Jameson.

"We are the chosen ones, but that's not so much an honor as it is a responsibility. Our task isn't to bring others into the fold, but to follow the Law, and most non Aztecs aren't interested." She then surprised me by opening a closet and bringing out a beautiful copy of the Law. It was a surprisingly large book that she held with great reverence. Jameson and I looked at each other with smiles, as memories of our first trip to Mexico flooded back. I particularly remembered Geraldo telling the story of the giving of the Ten Commandments, then frowned inside when I realized the story was told at the beach at Playa Del Carmen rather than at Cerro Raxon mountain.

Sol asked, "Do you have any copies of the Prophets?

"No. These are very expensive, and we're a small worship community. Between the Law, the Prophets, and the Writings, Aztecs most highly honor the Law, so we were honored to have this copy donated to us. That's the same with the Megillot. Another family blessed us with that gift."

The Value of the Empire

This time my mind went to our second trip to Mexico, when we sought to experience the Prophets. I had to quickly stop myself, because I am supposed to be learning about the Writings. We then went into a small auditorium, and Atzi said, "This is where we spend most of our time. We have special events here, and we collect most of our missional items in this area to box up and send out."

"So, you do mission, but not evangelism?" asked Jameson.

"That's right."

"Hmm," said Jameson. "Sounds an awful lot like many of the Caldwellian Churches I know. The one we attend in Phoenix has a wonderful missional program, but the thought of someone taking 'my seat' in the sanctuary, seems to outweigh any desire for evangelism. It got so bad, that our bishop sent out an email suggesting that evangelism and mission were two sides of the same coin, and both need to be practiced." Atzi seemed uninterested, but Jameson added one more thought. "The bishop later chastised our Arizona congregations for complaining too much. He suggested we put on an apron to serve rather than a bib to be served."

"So," said Atzi, "it sounds like putting mission and evangelism together is a great theory, but challenging to put into practice."

Solomon

With that sad thought, we headed to the third window to hear about Solomon. Atzi explained, "This book goes by several names: the Song of Solomon, the Song of Songs, or the Canticle of Canticles. They mean 'the best of the best,' but I just like to call it Solomon. Nobody knows who wrote it, but a very common understanding is that it is a celebration of God's love for God's people. What do you think it's about?"

"Sex," declared Jameson.

Sol was embarrassed, I wasn't surprised, and Atzi said, "Well, maybe. I think of it more about passionate love. Our priest even did a wedding homily from Solomon for two people who truly burned inside to be together. Some say the book is an allegory, which goes back to that common understanding. Others suggest it is cultic, with pagan religious rites, and nature myths that celebrate the seasons. It is also commonly seen as a drama, with characters and a plot, or an Aztec wedding song, or simply a secular piece of love poetry."

"What do you think it's about?" asked Sol.

"Oh, I certainly see it as symbolic, but that's what makes it fun. You can read this book from many different angles and get something new out of it every time. Another thing I love about this book is that it complemented the quite different language of law and prophecy."

"Why was it included in the final canonization of the Aztec Scriptures?" I asked.

"The answer is probably in the purpose of the song, and that has never been agreed upon. Isn't that one of the fun things about the Bible? It's openness to interpretation allows it to breathe new life into each generation."

Sol smiled and said, "My early years are beginning to come alive in good ways. Thanks, Atzi."

"Now let me do one of those things I like to do, and that's to give a quick preview of the book. Chapter 1 is a dialogue of the lovers. Chapter 2 has the lover arriving in spring. Chapter 3 is a wedding procession of the bridegroom. In chapter 4, the bridegroom praises the bride, and in the fifth chapter, the maiden dreams of finding her lover. Chapter 6 returns to the groom's praise of the bride's beauty, while chapter 7 lists the maiden's charms and her love is offered, and the final chapter expresses the desire for marriage.

"Okay. Ready to delve into the passion that is the book of Solomon?" All three of us looked mildly like deer caught in headlights, which is what I think she wanted. "Here's how it gets started, 'Let him kiss me with the kisses of his mouth! For your love is better than wine' (1:2)

"That's how God and the Mexican people relate?" asked a rather stunned Jameson.

"Well, first of all, it's symbolic, and second that's just one of the ways to think of it. Maybe this will help. Think of it like C. S. Lewis' *Chronicles of Narnia*. You can take it at face value or find many more layers. Next, the bride seeks a tryst. 'Tell me, you whom my soul loves, where you pasture your flock, where you make it lie down at noon' (1:7).

"I'm not catching the tryst thing here," said Jameson.

"It's artful. He would be resting at noon with his flock, making it a convenient time to get together. Use your imagination," Atzi said with a slightly devilish look. The groom responds with, 'Ah, you are beautiful, my beloved, truly beautiful' (1:16) I imagine he has just removed her clothes."

"Wow," said Sol with some minor frustration. "Jim Caldwell never talked like that."

"But he loved God, right?" asked Atzi.

"Of course," I offered, trying to settle things down, "because Jim went about trying to get people to understand God better."

"Now you're sounding like Ecclesiastes," said Sol.

"Next, the bride reminisces about her groom, 'The voice of

my beloved! Look, he comes, leaping upon the mountains, bounding over the hills' (2:8).

Sol said, "That's easier to take. She truly loves her beloved."

"To be honest," Jameson said, "that's not where my mind went."

Atzi was pleased, and said, "Yes! Just allow the story to touch you where you need." Jameson looked embarrassed as she continued. Chapter 3 begins with, 'Upon my bed at night I sought him whom my soul loves; I sought him, but found him not; I called him, but he gave no answer' (vs. 1)."

"Now that," said Sol, "is much easier to see as a story between God and God's people. Loving God, seeking God, and not finding God, is something I can relate to."

"Not so for chapter 4," continued Atzi. "'Your two breasts are like two fawns, twins of a gazelle, that feed among the lilies' (vs. 5).

I suggested that it could be a pagan ritual, because "it sounds like a celebration of undefiled nature."

"Okay," said Atzi, "try this. 'My beloved thrust his hand into the opening, and my inmost being yearned for him' (5:4)."

"Help me again," said Sol. "How did this make it into the Aztec Scriptures?"

"Passion, war, blood, and prostitutes elsewhere. Why not this?"

I said, "I'm talking it as secular love poem."

Atzi continued, "When she is asked what is so special about her lover, she says, 'His speech is most sweet, and he is altogether desirable. This is my beloved and this is my friend' (5:16)."

"Now that rings true for me," said Jameson, "as a

description of God."

"Chapter 6 is about the groom extolling the bride's beauty, like, 'Turn away your eyes from me, for they overwhelm me!' (vs. 5).

Jameson said, "Explain that one to me, please. I want it to be about Mexico and God, so what does it mean?"

"Ah!" said Atzi, 'you are discovering the beauty of poetry."

Jameson looked at me and said, "I thought we did that for the book of Psalms."

"Yes," I responded, "but Atzi's point is that poetry can have more than one interpretation."

She then continued, "Chapter 7 is a dialogue between the two lovers. He says, 'How fair and pleasant you are, O loved one, delectable maiden!' (vs. 6). She responds with, 'I am my beloved's, and his desire is for me' (vs. 10)."

Jameson said, "Wouldn't it be nice if the Caldwellian Church felt God's desire like that?"

"But the church, my son, is the people," said Sol, "and Solomon can also be seen as a poem about Jim Caldwell and the Church."

"The closing chapter says, 'I adjure you, O daughters of Tenochtitlan, do not stir up or awaken love until it is ready!' (8:4), then the bride offers this stirring testimony to the power of love:

> 'Set me as a seal upon your heart,
>   as a seal upon your arm;
>   for love is strong as death,
>   passion as fierce as the grave.
>   Its flashes are flashes of fire,
>   a raging flame.
>   Many waters cannot quench love,

neither can floods drown it.
If one offered for love
all the wealth of his house,
it would be utterly scorned'
(vv. 6-7)."

"Any questions?"
Jameson said, "More than I want to admit."

Esther

We laughed for a bit, then moved to the next display window. Atzi immediately removed the book for our perusal, and Jameson asked, "Why didn't you take Solomon out for us to see?"

"Ah, the treasures of love are always somewhat hidden," Atzi said with another impish grin. "Even old movies and television shows never showed sex. It was certainly implied, but in my opinion, today we leave nothing to the imagination. Leaving the book inaccessible was my offering of poetry." We then took the book back to a room and sat down. "Esther is the only book in the Bible that never mentions God."

"I have to ask," said a surprised Sol. "How in the world did it make it into the sacred scriptures?"

"Unfortunately, we don't have those responsible for the decision. They aren't alive, so we have no one to ask. In my opinion, its value comes in accomplishing divine will, even when God is silent. Let me once again do a book preview. Chapter 1 is a banquet given by King Ahasuerus, and the subsequent fall of Queen Vashti. The second chapter is the selection of Queen

The Value of the Empire

Esther. In chapter 3, Haman bribes King Ahasuerus to destroy the dispersed Aztecs. Chapter 4 has Mordecai inciting mourning. In chapter five, the King and Haman dine with Esther, while in the next chapter, Mordecai is honored by the King. In chapter 7, Esther is granted the hanging of Haman, and in the eighth chapter, the edict for the killing of the Aztecs is revoked. Chapter 9 has the Aztecs killing those who were going to kill them, and the last chapter sees Mordecai become popular.

"As we get started, let me also say that I take this book as a novel which addresses the question of how an Aztec should live in society. The tale probably originated in Persia, because Esther is the Aztec name of the Persian goddess Ishtar, and Mordecai means worshipper of Marduk, also a Persian god. I think the story was transposed into an Aztec novel to speak to the dispersed Aztecs after the exile. It reflected nationalistic pride when antagonism toward Gentiles ran high among Aztecs. It also purported to give the historical basis for the Festival of Purim: 'These days should be remembered and kept throughout every generation, in every family, province, and city; and these days of Purim should never fall into disuse among the Aztecs, nor should the commemoration of these days cease among their descendants' (9:28)."

"I'm getting mixed up between Spain and Persia," commented Jameson.

"Yes," said Atzi, "it's a bit confusing. The Aztecs were exiled to Spain, then Cyrus of Persia conquered the Spaniards and allowed the Aztecs to return home to Mexico. What happened was that some Aztecs remained in Spain, some went to Mexico, and some went to Persia, among other places. The story of Esther takes place in the Persian Empire during the reign of Ahasuerus. It features a young Aztec orphan who becomes the

The Value of the Empire

Persian queen. Along with her cousin Mordecai, they rescue the Aztecs from a genocidal plot by Haman.

"When you read this book as a dramatic play, you begin to catch the four characteristics of narrative: comedy is written to cause the audience to laugh; tragedy is the opposite of comedy as it deals with catastrophe; romance is about the fulfilment of dreams; irony happens when the audience's expectations don't happen. Irony is the main theme in this book. The orphan Esther becomes a queen, and the antagonist Haman becomes the victim. Any questions?"

Sol asked, "What does Haman mean? I've known a few people with that last name."

"Funny you should ask. All of the characters in this play have meaning behind their name except Haman. That's because biblical scholars are uncertain what it means. So, here we go." She turned to the first page of the book, and said, "After two banquets were served up by King Ahasuerus, with plenty of heavy drinking, Queen Vashti gave a banquet for the women. On the seventh day, when the king was pretty much drunk out of his mind, the king commanded that the queen be brought to him. She refused and the king was enraged. The queen had wronged the king, and that didn't sit too well with him. After consulting many people, he discovered that disobedience was against the law and it was unalterable. It was then decided to give her position to another, so that all women would learn from this, and give honor to their husbands."

"Sounds pretty patristic," said Jameson.

Sol chimed in, "not to mention chauvinistic."

"Of course! Too bad the world hasn't learned any better by now. Shouldn't a play turn people around?" The three of us looked at each other, and agreed, then she said, "The first chapter ends with a declaration that every man should be master in his own house."

"There you go again," said Sol.

Jameson said, "That doesn't fly too well today."

Atzi said, "Trust me. It only gets worse. The way the story goes, the king's servants suggest he find a beautiful young virgin."

"What's wrong with that?" asked Jameson.

"Because the servants paraded all the beautiful young virgins before the king, after they were fancied up with cosmetic treatments."

Jameson said, "Still not seeing a problem."

"Oh, my heavens!" complained Atzi. "If the only requirement to become queen is to be young and beautiful, then the story is objectifying women."

"Oops, sorry," he said, as his mother looked disapprovingly at him.

"The problem improves because an Aztec man named Mordecai had a cousin named Esther. He adopted and raised her when her parents died, and she was collected up into the harem at the king's palace after a raid. There she gained favor and quickly advanced to the best place in the harem."

Sol asked, "Did it matter that she was an Aztec?"

"It would have. That's why Mordecai told her to keep it a secret. He also walked by the front of the court of the harem every day to see how Esther was doing. After a year of preparation, a select group of women were presented to the king. One at a time they spent the night with the king, and would only return if invited. When Esther was summoned, she asked for nothing. Now the king ended up loving Esther more than the others, so she was crowned as queen, replacing Vashti.

The Value of the Empire

"That brings us to Mordecai. One day he was sitting at the king's gate, and heard two guards conspiring to assassinate the king. As the Queen's stepfather, he had access to Esther, so he let her know the terrible news. Esther told the king, in the name of Mordecai, and the matter was investigated. When it was found to be true, the two guards were abruptly hanged on the gallows in the public square. Mordecai did this favor for the king, but asked for nothing, just like Esther had done previously. Nonetheless, Mordecai was surprised that the king showed no appreciation.

"Five years later, a man named Haman rose through the king's ranks, and the servants were commanded by the king to bow to Haman. One day, Haman became infuriated when Mordecai refused to bow to him, and the matter was investigated. When Haman discovered that Mordecai was an Aztec, he plotted to destroy all the Aztecs in the kingdom. He told the king that the Aztecs in his kingdom followed other laws, so the king granted permission to have the Aztecs destroyed. Letters were sent to all of the provinces to kill every Aztec, in one day, and to plunder their goods. When all of the people were called upon to be ready for the day, the king and Haman sat down to a celebration banquet. The problem was that the people of the kingdom found the decree to be confusing."

"As all heinous crimes should be," stated a rather angry Sol, with her arms folded.

"Agreed," said Atzi, "and the story fortunately improves. Esther's maids told her the terrible news, and showed her a copy of the decree. Esther was not allowed to approach the king without an invitation, so Mordecai got word to her that it would be wrong for her to keep silence at such a time as this. Esther told Mordecai to use this time of confusion to pray, and then she

The Value of the Empire

would approach the king. Esther said that it was strictly against the law of the country, but she was willing to die for her people if necessary.

Esther got adorned in her royal robes, and stood in view of the king. He was sitting on his royal throne and saw his queen, and decided to allow her to approach. He asked what she wanted, and Esther invited the king and Haman to a banquet she had prepared. While drinking wine, the king asked Esther again what she wanted. Esther surprised both Haman and the king by issuing yet another invitation to a banquet. The caveat was that the king was becoming further indebted to grant her request.

"Haman departed with a smile on his face, not knowing the confusion being observed in the kingdom, rather than the decree. When he saw Mordecai, Haman was again infuriated because Mordecai continued his refusal to bow. Haman went home and bragged about his accomplishments, his invitation to join the king in a private banquet put on by Esther, and another invitation for tomorrow. He then complained about the Aztec Mordecai, and his wife suggested a gallows be made to hang him.

"That night the king couldn't sleep, so he decided to do some reading in the royal archives. He discovered that Mordecai was the one who alerted the king's guards about his assassination conspiracy. He called a servant in and asked how Mordecai was rewarded, and found that nothing had been done. That morning Haman arrived to tell the king his plan to have Mordecai hanged on the gallows, but the king spoke first. 'What shall be done for the man whom the king wishes to honor?' Haman thought the man he talked about must surely be himself, so he says,

The Value of the Empire

'Let royal robes be brought, which the king has worn and a horse that the king has ridden, with a royal crown on its head. Let the robes and the horse be handed over to one of the king's most noble officials; let him robe the man whom the king wishes to honor, and let him conduct the man on horseback through the open square of the city, proclaiming before him: Thus shall it be done for the man whom the king wishes to honor' (Esther 6:8-9).

"I'm sensing potential irony here," said Jameson with a smile.

Atzi nodded and went on. "The king was delighted by Haman's thoughtful plan, and told him to go and do as he suggested for the Aztec Mordecai. Haman was beyond shocked, but he had to obey the king, so he honored Mordecai as instructed. When the parade was done, Haman went home in shame and mourned. A knock at the door was heard, and it was the king's servants coming to take him to the second banquet planned by Esther. Soon the king arrived at the banquet by Queen Esther, with a rather downcast Haman.

"On the second day, as they freely partook of wine, the king once again offered to grant any request the Queen had. She shocked the king when she requested that she and her people not be killed. The king angrily asked who was planning to kill her people, and she said, 'Haman.' The king got up and left in a fit of rage, while Haman begged for his life from the Queen. When the king returned, he saw Haman far too close to his Queen, and he yelled out that Haman was assaulting her. One of the king's servants mentioned that Haman had constructed a gallows for Mordecai, so the king ordered the execution of Haman on his own gallows.

The Value of the Empire

"Irony fulfilled," said Sol.

"Oh, there's more. In an ironic twist of fate, the king gave Esther the house of Haman, and she told the king that Mordecai was her cousin. Mordecai was told to immediately report to the king, so he went with no little bit of trepidation. Standing before the king, he was shocked to see the king remove his signet ring and hand it to him. Esther then pleaded to the king to avert the evil that Haman had devised against the Aztecs. She explained that she could not live with herself if her people were destroyed. The king told her that she could write a letter to her people in any way she wanted, sign his name to it, and seal it with the signet ring.

"The edict was written to the Aztecs, and all of the officials of his kingdom. Letters were then delivered by riders on the king's fastest steeds, and the Aztecs were told that they could take revenge on their enemies. In every city there was gladness and joy among the Aztecs, and they had a festival and a holiday. Their joy was even greater because the very day they were to be destroyed, was the day they were allowed to take revenge. To everyone's surprise, the Aztecs chose not to slaughter. The day turned from mourning into gladness, and the festival was called Purim."

Atzi said, "That's four stories down and one to go. What do you think so far of the Megillot?"

"I like," Sol offered, "the variety of their contexts. Correct me if I'm wrong, but I think Lamentations was set in Mexico after the deportees returned, as was Ecclesiastes. Solomon was a timeless song, and Esther was set in Persia during the Dispersion."

Jameson said, "I like their association with festivals. Pretty cool that Ecclesiastes can be celebrated by remembering the tent camping hard times of wandering in the wilderness. Esther is used at the Feast of Purim, and Lamentations is read on the date of the destruction of the Temple in Tenochtitlan, but I forget Solomon's purpose."

Atzi said, "It's used at the Passover Feast."

"Oh, that's why I was confused. I thought Jim Caldwell started Passover."

"Not uncommon," said Atzi. "Most Caldwellians, at least in my experience, think Pentecost was started by Jim." I asked which festival it was read at, and she said, "Ruth. It's read during the celebration of the giving of the Law."

"Oh, I get it," I said. "Aztecs celebrate the Law coming down on Mount Cerro, just like Caldwellians celebrate the Spirit coming down on the Hole in the Rock Gang."

Sol and Jameson still looked confused, so Atzi said, "Both religions call those experiences Pentecost, which comes from the word *pente* and means fifty. The Aztec Pentecost happens fifty days after Passover, while the Caldwellian Pentecost is celebrated fifty days after Easter."

"Nope," said Jameson, "sorry. No help."

Sol said it was starting to bring back a few memories from her childhood, so Atzi said, "Just let it sink in. This is good for Aztecs and Caldwellians to learn more about one another's faith traditions. That brings us to the final book of the Megillot."

Ruth

We walked down to the last window, where the four chapters of Ruth were displayed on four pages and in full view. Atzi didn't take the fragile pages out, so we stood back and listened to the story. I couldn't help but look into the glass and see our reflection. I know I was supposed to see through the glass and listen to Atzi talk about the book of Ruth, but the idea of reflecting on our own past was very tempting.

Any hope of that was shattered as she began. "First of all, who do you think is the main character?"

Jameson said, "Sounds like a trick question, but I'll still say Ruth."

"No," said Atzi, with an almost fiendish gleam in her eyes. "That was a trick question." We all laughed, then she said, "It's Naomi. The Caldwellian Scriptures place this book right after the book of Judges, to set its context at a time when there was no king in Mexico. The reason was to let it pave the way for King Montezuma, whose great-grandmother was Ruth. The Aztec Scriptures include it among the Writings part of the Bible, because the attitudes of the major characters in Ruth fit a post-exilic mindset.

"This book showed that the LORD was concerned for people of every nation. It helped counter the opinion in the Aztec religion that said marriage to foreigners was wrong, like in Ezra and Nehemiah. Another purpose seems to be about redemption. Variations of the word show up 20 times in the 85 verses of the book.

"The plot focuses on Naomi, an Aztec, and her Honduran daughter-in-law, Ruth. Here's my traditional preview of the book. Chapter 1 is about Ruth deciding to leave her homeland to return with her mother-in-law to San Miguel Ajusco, just south of modern day Mexico City. In Chapter 2, Ruth finds favor with a man named Boaz, and in the third chapter, Ruth and Boaz become engaged. In Chapter 4, Ruth marries Boaz. To add a little flavor, here's the meaning of the characters:

The Value of the Empire

Elimelech means my God is King.
Naomi means my joy.
Mahlon means weakening.
Chilion means pining.
Orpah means cloud.
Ruth means water abundantly.
Boaz means quickening.

"Okay, ready to get started?" We all nodded a yes, so Atzi began. "One day, a famine in the land became unbearable. A certain man of San Miguel Ajusco went to live in the country of Honduras, he and his wife and two sons. The name of the man was Elimelech, the name of his wife was Naomi, and the names of his two sons were Mahlon and Chilion. They went to the Honduras and remained there. Elimelech died and Naomi was left with her two sons. They took Honduran wives named Orpah and Ruth. About ten years later, both Mahlon and Chilion died.

"Naomi started to return to Mexico with her daughters-in-law from Honduras, because she heard that the famine was over. However, Naomi insisted that Orpah and Ruth stay and return to their mother's houses. Then she kissed them and they all wept aloud. They insisted on continuing with her, but Naomi begged them to turn back. Finally, Orpah agreed to stay in Honduras, but Ruth clung to her. Naomi tried one more time to talk some sense into Ruth, but Ruth said,

'Do not press me to leave you
or to turn back from following you!
Where you go, I will go;
where you lodge, I will lodge;
your people shall be my people,

The Value of the Empire

and your God my God.
Where you die, I will die—
there will I be buried.
May the LORD do thus and so to me,
and more as well,
if even death parts me from you!'

"When Naomi saw how determined Ruth was, she said nothing more about it. So the two of them traveled along until they reached San Miguel Ajusco. When they arrived, the whole town was stirred up. They asked, 'Are you Naomi?' She said, 'Yes, but now please call me Mara, for the Almighty has dealt bitterly with me. I went away full, but the LORD brought me back empty.'"

Jameson said, "I'll bet that didn't sit too well with Ruth!"

"Probably not, but things started to get better. Now Naomi had a relative whose name was Boaz. Ruth said to Naomi, 'Let me go to the field and glean, in hopes of being seen by someone who might favor me.' Naomi gave her blessing and Ruth went. As it happened, she came to the part of the field belonging to Boaz. When he saw her, he inquired about her, and discovered she was the Honduran who had returned with Naomi."

Sol asked, "Why is it that the story continues to refer to her as Naomi, rather than the requested name of Mara?"

"Good observation," said Atzi. "I don't know. But Ruth had been toiling all day without a moment's rest. Boaz went to Ruth and told her to work only in his field. He said, 'I have ordered the young men not to bother you. If you get thirsty, drink from what the young men have drawn. I have heard all that you have done for your mother-in-law, and that you left your native land

and came to a people you did not know. May the LORD reward you for your deeds.' Ruth replied, 'May I continue to find favor in your sight, my lord, for you have comforted me.' At mealtime, Boaz offered her some bread and food. She ate until she was full and she had some left over."

"That reminds me of the time Jim Caldwell fed the multitudes," said Jameson, "and they had bread left over."

Atzi continued, "Boaz further instructed the young men to leave extra grain in the field for her, and to not rebuke her. That evening she came into town and Naomi saw how much she had gleaned. Naomi asked her where she had gleaned, and she told her it was in the fields of Boaz. Naomi said that he was a relative, and both women were pleased. Ruth was living with her mother-in-law, so they returned home that night.

"In the morning, Naomi suggested that Ruth should seek some sort of security for her future. She told Naomi that Boaz would be winnowing barley at the threshing floor that night, so she should put on her best clothes and go down to the threshing floor. She said, 'When he lies down, go uncover him and lie down; he will tell you what to do.'"

"Is this a sex scene?" asked Jameson, to the disgruntlement of his mother.

"Ah," said Atzi, "you have again found the joy of storytelling. It doesn't have to mean what it says, but it can certainly mean what it means."

"What do you mean?" asked Jameson.

Atzi said, "Fill in your own blanks. Anyway, our task is to listen to the story. When Boaz had eaten and drunk, he went to lie down at the end of the heap of grain. Ruth stealthily approached, uncovered him, and lay down. At midnight he woke up and was startled, and asked who it was lying with him.

The Value of the Empire

She told him it was Ruth, and he complimented her because the townsfolk knew she was a worthy woman. He then told her to lie down until the morning.

"The next day, Boaz gathered the people of the town and said, 'Today you are witnesses that I have acquired from the hand of Naomi all that belonged to Elimelech. I have also acquired Ruth.' Then all of the people said that they were witnesses, and offered blessings. So Boaz took Ruth and she became his wife. When they came together, the LORD made her conceive, and she bore a son. They named him Obed, and he became the father of Jesse, the father of King Montezuma."

"In the Caldwellian faith," I said, "we refer to Jim Caldwell as having come from the house and lineage of King Montezuma."

"Yes," said Atzi, "and that is one thing that separates your faith from the Aztec faith."

"In what way?" asked Sol.

Atzi said, "Our faith is looking for a messiah who will come and bring peace on earth. I look around and don't see that has happened yet."

Sol said, "I agree with you, but the important thing is that Jim Caldwell brings peace within."

Atzi smiled and said, "I have another tour group coming soon, so I need to get ready. At that point, Atzi walked us to the front door and thanked us for our interest. Sol gave her a hug, and Jameson and I thanked her for her time and we departed.

"Before going home," asked Jameson, "can we stop for lunch?" When I asked where, he said, "Fat Olives." I thought it was a great idea. Not only was it right on our way along Route 66, but we had plenty of time to catch the lunch specials. Soon enough we were pulling into the small parking lot for Fat Olives

The Value of the Empire

Wood-Fired Pizzeria and Italian Kitchen. Sol never requests Mexican food, because she's spoiled on her mother's cooking. Being a week day, we got right in and seated. They are famous for their authentic thin crust, wood-fired Neapolitan pizza, but everything is good.

We got our menus and started salivating. The server came by quickly and I decided to spring for an appetizer. I ordered a classic bruschetta board, then asked everyone to be ready to order when it arrived. Meeting the task at hand, Sol was first. She requested a smoked salmon sandwich, Jameson went for the margherita pizza, and I chose their signature lasagna.

After a great meal, we started back down I-17 toward Phoenix.

"Hey, mom."

"Hey, son."

"Why don't we finish the story after Ruth? Would you please read Matthew 1:6-16?"

Sol gladly picked up her Bible and quite solemnly read:

> Montezuma was the father of Santiago,
> Santiago was the father of Rehoboam,
> Rehoboam the father of Abijah,
> Abijah the father of Asa,
> Asa the father of Jehoshaphat,
> Jehoshaphat the father of Jehoram,
> Jehoram the father of Uzziah,
> Uzziah the father of Jotham,
> Jotham the father of Ahaz,
> Ahaz the father of Hezekiah,
> Hezekiah the father of Manasseh,
> Manasseh the father of Amon,

The Value of the Empire

Amon the father of Josiah,
and Josiah the father of Jeconiah.
After the exile to Spain:
Jeconiah was the father of Shealtiel,
Shealtiel the father of Zerubbabel,
Zerubbabel the father of Abihud,
Abihud the father of Eliakim,
Eliakim the father of Azor,
Azor the father of Zadok,
Zadok the father of Akim,
Akim the father of Elihud,
Elihud the father of Eleazar,
Eleazar the father of Matthan,
Matthan the father of Jacob,
and Jacob the father of Joseph,
the husband of Mary,
and Mary was the mother of Jim Caldwell
who is called the Messiah.

She serenely closed her Bible and Jameson and I thanked her. "Now tell us," requested Jameson, "how Jim Caldwell ended up in Phoenix."

"Oh, that's easy. You just need the last name of Joseph, the husband of Mary."

"Please remind me," said Jameson.

"Joseph's last name was Calderon, and his wife's name was Maria. During the Mexican-American War, which ended in 1848, the U.S. gained control of the Phoenix area. In 1851, Jim Calderon was born to Joseph and Maria. The Gadsden Purchase of 1854 was a treaty that gave $10 million dollars to Mexico for land south of the Phoenix area, where Joseph, Maria

The Value of the Empire

and Jim lived. This made them United States citizens, so Maria started going by Mary, and Joseph changed his last name from Calderon to Caldwell."

When we pulled into our driveway, I was beyond ecstatic to have experienced the three parts of the Aztec Bible in such a unique way. I'll never be able to read it the same again, because now I will connect the stories to the sights and sounds of the area. As we got out of the car, I hugged my wife and thanked her for joining us on this particular trip, not to mention the second trip to Mexico. Then I gave my son a hug and thanked him for allowing me to participate in his original high school graduation gift that paved the way for the remainder of our journeys.

As I got back in the house, I saw my copy of *The Four Agreements* given to me so long ago by Maria, who helped me plan the trips. She also asked me to live with my understandings, so I reflected back on the excursions. All of a sudden it started coming together. The poetry of the Psalms were wonderful examples of the first agreement: Be Impeccable with Your Word. I decided right then and there to live my life in a more poetic way, by loosening my self-imposed strictures of agenda. It takes time to find the words that truly express oneself, and then becoming a person who keeps your word.

The wisdom expressed in Proverbs and Job became an illustration for me of the second agreement: Don't Take Things Personally. That will be a monumental challenge, because my ego is fragile. The next time I feel confronted, I'll remember Job. He dealt with a divine attack and came out the better for it. Then there's Proverbs. I realized I needed to absorb more of its wisdom, so I opened my Bible and read the opening verses. This caught my attention: "Let the wise also hear and gain in learning, and the discerning acquire skill" (1:5). Lord, help me to gain the skills needed to not take things personally.

The storytelling was a unique experience. It helped me gain new appreciations for Ezra, Nehemiah, Chronicles, and Daniel. As I looked back again at the agreements, the third one says: Don't Make Assumptions. The hidden agenda of Chronicles taught me to research carefully, so I wouldn't get caught assuming what a biblical book is about. The same goes for Daniel. I've never been interested in an—or *the*—apocalypse, but my assumption about it was all wrong. It is full of useful lessons about life here and now.

The close encounter with the Megillot was very revealing. I never knew how the Aztecs used Lamentations, Ecclesiastes, Solomon, Esther, and Ruth. The fourth agreement: Always Do Your Best, taught me openness, so I could get a greater appreciation of Jim Caldwell's roots. I hope I can practice what Maria preached about living the agreements. It helps to bridge the gap between scripture and life. Most importantly, the Aztec Scriptures and the Caldwellian Scriptures give us some idea of what it was like to experience God. That became my prayer: that people would be open to the many ways people experience God, and to know that we are all God's people.

Shakespeare wrote: "All the world's a stage, and all the men and women merely players." My Old Testament trilogy is offered as a play, and it is now complete. May our lives be more than merely players, but movers and shakers, toward the task of leaving this world better than when we arrived.

The Value of the Empire

If you want to read about the Caldwellian Bible, check out my fictional trilogy about the New Testament, comprising the Jim Caldwell Trilogy.

ACKNOWLEDGMENTS

The *New Revised Standard Version* (NRSV) of *The Holy Bible* is used throughout this book when texts are referenced.

Many thanks to Dave Raines, who shines in proof reading, where I am dull.

My heartfelt gratitude to my wife and life companion, Yvonne Cuenca Oropeza. Her copyediting suggestions made this book much better than it would have been without her. She graciously hand-drew the pictures of the buildings at the beginning of each Act.

Finally, my thanks to God, who's been with me throughout the many Acts and Scenes of my life.

BOOKS BY THIS AUTHOR

Nonfiction

A Natural History of Scripture: How the Bible Evolved— Book 1.

This is the first book in my serious, in-depth, Bible Study trilogy, written for those who want to get serious about the Bible. It is a deconstruction of biblical formation as seen through the lens of evolutionary biology.

Wrestling with Scripture: How to Interpret the Bible— Book 2.

This is the second book in my trilogy, written for those who want to know what a particular word means in its own setting. It shows how to interpret the Bible's original Greek and Hebrew by using word study tools.

Practicing Scripture: How to Live the Bible— Book 3.

This is the third book in my trilogy, calling upon my Doctoral work in Practical Theology. It explains how to put the ideas from the Bible into every day practice.

The Value of the Empire

How to Lead a Celebration of Life

This is an indispensable guide, built on my 37-year career as a pastor, teaching laity and clergy how to conduct a funeral with meaning and integrity.

Don't Look a Camel in the Mouth: Pilgrimages through the Land of Jesus and Paul

This book shares five pilgrimages I led with my wife through the Holy Land, Turkey, Greece, Italy, and the Mediterranean. It brings the Bible alive through storytelling from a modern perspective.

Don't Look a Camel in the Mouth: Includes Journal

This book begins with *Don't Look a Camel in the Mouth: Pilgrimages through the Land of Jesus and Paul*, and ends with a Journal that contains spiritual questions and space to reflect on them with your own answers.

Parish the Thought: An Eye-Opening Look Behind the Pulpit

This book is a candid look at the joys and concerns of pulpit ministry. In it, my wife and I share stories of our years as ordained clergy.

The Value of the Empire

Austria, Germany, and the Oberammergau Passion Play

This book shared the experiences my wife and I had taking a group to the famous Oberammergau Passion Play, and our adventures through the surrounding region.

Your Year of Spiritual Growth: A Biblical Journey

This book is designed for people who love to journal. It creates spirituality through daily scripture readings, devotional questions, and debriefing with others.

Building a Bridge Over a Broken World: A Memoir

???

Fiction

The Forming of the Diamond: A Jim Caldwell Story—Book 1

This is the first book in my New Testament historical biblical fiction trilogy. It is a retelling of the life of Jesus, drawn from the four gospels, looking through the lens of the American Old

The Value of the Empire

West. It focuses on The Sermon on the Mount, and shares some of the parables and healings from Jesus' ministry.

The Secret of the Diamond: A Jim Caldwell Story— Book 2

This middle book of my Jim Caldwell trilogy is a creative reimagining of the last days of Jesus, set in Phoenix in 1881. It deals with the Passion Narrative, from Gethsemane to the grave, which I call the diamond of the Gospel.

The Value of the Diamond: A Jim Caldwell Story— Book 3

This final book of my biblical fiction trilogy deals with the resurrection, and tells what the early church's mission might have looked like if set in Mexico and the American West. It share the Good News from the Book of Acts and the Letters of Paul, and ends with the Book of Revelation.

The Secret of the Diamond: A Lenten Devotional

This booklet coordinates with *The Secret of the Diamond: A Jim Caldwell Story: Book 2*, and is designed for spiritual growth during Lent.

The Value of the Empire

The Jim Caldwell Trilogy

This is a combination of all three books of the Jim Caldwell series.

The Forming of the Empire: A King Montezuma Story— Book 1

This is the first book in my Old Testament biblical historical fiction trilogy. It is a reimagining of the Law section of the Hebrew Scriptures, through the book of Kings. It is set in the Formative and Classic Periods of Mesoamerica, beginning in the jungles of Guatemala and ending in what is now Mexico City.

The Secret of the Empire: A King Montezuma Story— Book 2

This middle book of my King Montezuma trilogy deals with the development of biblical prophecies. The Aztec Empire ended when Hernan Cortés and the Spanish Conquistadors overthrew Mexico. The book reimagines the Prophets section of the Hebrew Scriptures by setting them in the Postclassic Period of Mesoamerica.

The Value of the Empire: A King Montezuma Story— Book 3

The Value of the Empire

This is the final book in my biblical fiction trilogy. It retells the Writings part of the Hebrew Scriptures, sharing the legends, wisdom, poetry, and stories left behind in Mexico. It also paves the way for the Jim Caldwell Trilogy.

The King Montezuma Trilogy

This as a combination of all three books of the King Montezuma series.

If you enjoy my books, please review them on Amazon, Goodreads, Barnes & Noble, or any of your favorite places.